Nation
Under
God

JAMES
LUALLEN

DENVER, COLORADO

Nation Under God
All Rights Reserved.
Copyright © 2012 James Luallen
v2.0

Outskirts Press, Inc.
http://www.outskirtspress.com

ISBN: 978-1-4327-8599-4

Library of Congress Control Number: 2012902579

Outskirts Press and the "OP" logo are trademarks belonging to Outskirts Press, Inc.

PRINTED IN THE UNITED STATES OF AMERICA

PROLOGUE

The USA eventually became a 'Christian Nation,' before the 22nd Century. This took until the mid-Twenty-
First Century; but, the DNA for what the USA would
finally become was inseminated by the Colonial Puritans.
They had been subjected to intolerance of their religious
beliefs and practices in Europe, and celebrated their new
freedom in America by establishing *a theocracy*. Historians
have well studied and documented just how tyrannical
and totalitarian EVERY theocratic 'civilization' in human
history became. A great number of atrocities, like those
committed among Puritans "In the name of God", happen to citizens under any theocracy – irrespective of the
source religion [Islam, Christian, etc.].

*Christian Puritanism deeply infected the DNA of the
USA*. The country never fully escaped the influence of the
Puritanical moralistic views regarding *SEXUAL PURITY.*
Sexual morality was given *special* attention by the Colonial
Puritans. The records tell of hundreds of colonial sinners
forced to sit in the stocks in public view for sexual im-
morality. For example, in 1656 Captain Kemble of Boston

was put in public stocks for two hours for his "lewd and unseemly behavior," which consisted of kissing his wife in public on the Sabbath on the doorstep of his house after his return from a three-year voyage.

After the U.S. Supreme Court, in 1973, published the ruling of *"Roe v Wade"*, the struggle began with renewed intensity. *"Roe v Wade"* seemed to punctuate the advancing civil rights movements of both feminism, and a sexual revolution. This was far too much for the descendants of Puritan morality. Whether the headliner was *"The National Right to Life"* organization, or *"Focus on the Family,"* the puritans of the so-called "religious right" in America kept up their pursuit of public policies that fit their biblical fundamentalism doctrine, for decade after decade after decade.

After the shocking psycho-social impact of the "9-11" attack in 2001, the cultural tendency of insecurity and paranoia in America became an all out hysterical drive for security in absolutes, and a patriarchal moral authority. An underlying hope of a return to "better days of the past", led the multitudes to lodge their moral and spiritual center in conservative fundamentalist Christian *{Puritan}* organizations in ever increasing numbers. What emerged in following years tipped the balance of the so-called "culture wars" of American society. The USA moved away from a separation of church and state, and toward a Christian theocracy; fully arriving there by 2073.

CHAPTER ONE

That Friday began for Rachel DeLine with dread anxiety over losing her job. What happened that day was not as bad as she had expected. It was far worse.

'Reverend Rachel' [as she was called by locals] directed a ministry of care-giving and education for new mothers at a nearby social services agency. In fact, she was the founder of the "Early Steps Center for Parenthood," in downtown Colorado Springs. The work she did for small children and their young mothers was popular; thus, giving her some local fame.

However, as a female clergyperson, she was a dinosaur at age thirty-eight.

Reverend Rachel was one of a breed headed for extinction that year – the Year of our Lord 2073. This was inevitable, as the new social order of the world's foremost Christian nation would not recognize the legitimacy of her ordination. Indeed, it could not. The Holy Bible dictated that women must not be leaders – and the federal government, now run by the National Christian Church, would soon require that Rachel be removed from her job.

All this was due to the recent ratification of *"The Holy Bible Standards"* Amendment to the U.S. Constitution. Her country was now absolutely a theocracy.

An impending meeting with Colorado Springs' city authorities consumed Rachel's thoughts as she pedaled her bicycle to work. The ride was only ten blocks, and the morning was typical for Colorado Springs in October: sunlit and pleasantly cool, without feeling cold. Yet Rachel's mood was unaffected by the glory of the new day, as she was rehearsing the interview she expected later that morning with the City Magistrate. The reassuring feel of the pedals under her feet kept her grounded in reality while she mentally ran through what she planned to say. She had no way to know whether she had prepared adequately…or if it were even possible to prepare adequately.

She punched the speed dial of her bike-mounted cellular phone, and rang her friend Martha, the lawyer. While listening to the phone ring in the earpiece of her helmet, she muttered a sub-verbal curse when she hit a bump in the bike path. Her balance faltered for a moment, but with the confidence gained from years of riding, she leveraged her strong legs, and continued onward without falling. She heard Martha's musical voice in her ear and her heart leapt with relief -- but it was a recorded message: "If you get this message, I have been called to the courtroom on this Friday to serve as a Public Defender. You can leave a message if you'd like. If your name is Rachel, I'm really sorry but this will prevent me from keeping our appointment – still, I had no choice. I'll phone you when I can. God Bless (beep)."

"Oh no," Rachel said aloud, as she banked her bike around the last corner of her route, pedaling up the block to the driveway of the Center. She calculated her other option for a "witness" to attend the meeting with her – her supervising Elder for the district, Eric Wilson. She braked carefully, trying not to stir up the gravel parking lot, but as always, a puff of dust heralded her arrival. Rachel reached for the cell phone to once again speed dial – but before she could complete the move, she saw the custodian on the doorstep, frantically waving her down. She smiled at him, and held up her index finger to indicate "one moment." Then she hastily dismounted, locked her bike to the railing of the handicapped ramp, and stepped up to greet Clarence, and to learn what he thought so urgent.

"Mornin', Rev," he said, then added, "That city feller from the television is here, and waiting for you inside." Clarence's pleasantly weathered face was worried, his brow knitted.

"Oh! Wow, Clarence -- the magistrate wasn't supposed to get here until the time I listed on the notice – nine o'clock!"

"I know, but he showed up a bit ago, when I was out here rakin' up some leaves, and he made it clear he was going to stay 'til you was here, and … well, I didn't come up with no way to make him come back, and so…"

"Of course, Clarence, you did the right thing. It's just that I'm surprised, and not sure how to…hey, Karen hasn't come in early, has she?"

"No -- not yet, anyway."

"Oh, well; it was just a thought," Rachel said. "So I guess I better just go on in and see him. Hmmm…where did you say he was waiting?"

"I left him in the resource room, Rev." He hesitated, opened his mouth as if he had something further to say, but then shut it again, shaking his head slightly, as if he were afraid that he would presume too far.

"Thanks, Clarence…I'll see you later." And she started to turn from him, reaching for the door, when she seemed to read his expression, so she paused. "What is it, Clarence?"

He cleared his throat and shifted his weight uneasily. "Uhh…it's just that, well, if this is…I mean, would you like me to come with you – just to sit and, you know, be there to listen along – too?"

Rachel looked at him, a smile lighting her face; he wasn't a lawyer, but he was a good, reliable man – and she knew he was on her side. "Say, you know what, Clarence?! That would be great! Thanks. So come on, let's go see 'The MAN'!" Still smiling up at him, Rachel held the door open, waving him in ahead of her. Then, with a sigh like a silent prayer of relief, she followed him in.

Church Elder and City Magistrate Jerry Cromwell served the Colorado Springs community as both the chief religious leader and the chief civil authority, because church and government were melded together. He was responsible for the social order and the moral health of the Colorado Springs "parish." Merely a glance at the fifty-eight-year-old man could give one the impression of his solidity, and his upright bearing: this was a man of substance. Whatever shortcomings Cromwell might have, frivolity was obviously not among them.

When they discovered the magistrate in her office, (not the resource room), it was clear to Rachel that Elder Cromwell was asserting his oversight authority into the Center, rather than visiting as a guest dignitary. His impeccable clothing made the humble office look even more plain in contrast; Rachel had acquired all the furniture second-hand, to focus her funds on program development and staff. She felt that his practiced eye took in every detail: the scratched fiberglass desktop, the dented filing cabinet, the slightly crooked window blinds. He took it in, and made it his own. Therefore it was not surprising that Cromwell took the initiative by speaking first, rising from his chair to do so. He nodded to her in a gesture of polite deference, but this was merely gentlemanly good manners. He was in charge, and they both knew it.

"Hello, Mrs. DeLine; I'm glad to see you. I thought this was about your usual time for arrival. Thank you for bringing her to me, Clarence -- and will you please close the door as you leave us?"

This had the intended effect upon them both, as Clarence silently froze in the doorway, while Rachel swallowed hard, struggling for a response. She heard the slight crack in her own voice as she forced out a reply.

"Uhm…if you please, your eminence, I've invited Clarence to sit with us while we have this meeting – as the witness that holy law permits me."

Cromwell tilted his head slightly to one side for a moment, considering; then he nodded again, this time in agreement. "Oh? I see. Well, I suppose that will be acceptable – although you're making this more formal than I had intended, Rachel. But you're certainly correct about the law on that point. Both of you may come in to join me -- and then close the door, won't you, Clarence?" And with those words, Cromwell resumed his seat, which just allowed room for Rachel to make her way past him, around the desk, to her own office chair. She felt self-conscious squeezing by him in the small space. Clarence closed the door, and then he pulled the only other chair in the small office toward himself, away from Cromwell's chair. Clarence sat with his arms folded and his expression fixed, clearly disapproving of Cromwell's ambush.

As she seated herself, Rachel began speaking. "Magistrate, I was under the impression, from the notice I'd received, that this would be a formal meeting, and that it was scheduled for about an hour from now, at nine o'clock. So, please forgive me if I've misunderstood, but that's why I may seem a bit awkward." She was reassured by the fluency of her own words, feeling that she had regained her composure enough to make a respectable impression.

As she spoke, Rachel studied the refined-looking man in the blue suit, looking back at her through wire-rimmed eyeglasses. She thought to herself that he could be any "mild-mannered reporter," except for the barely perceptible air of almost regal authority he exuded. And he was staring back at her with grey eyes that were alert and observant, but which did not reveal any of the thoughts or feelings behind them. She kept her own face as impassive as she could; she knew her "poker face" was not very good.

"Rachel," he began, "Let me assure you that while I am calling on you regarding an official matter, these are not official proceedings – if they were, well, we'd be meeting at my office, instead – and there would be a few others in attendance. So, if you'll allow me, I'd like to share with you a decision regarding your community leadership – in as casual and friendly a manner as I may." At that point, he paused with the question in his eyebrows, waiting for her assent. When she nodded, he resumed. "As you know, the Holy Bible Standards Amendment to the U.S. Constitution has numerous ramifications for local governance and local organizations, many of which we are only now beginning to implement. One of those Biblical principles for the organization of church agencies will soon be applied to you and this excellent little ministry center. You know the matter I refer to, I assume – that the Bible ordains only men should direct and supervise any ministries of the church?"

She wondered if he could sense the surge of disappointment that twisted her stomach whenever she thought about this – her visceral reaction to the injustice of the law. "Yes, Magistrate, I'm aware of that issue."

Assuming a fatherly expression, almost with a look of regret on his face, Cromwell said, "Rachel, I can only guess how difficult this must be for you to accept – after all, you have done admirable work in getting this operation created from nothing. You've shown tremendous leadership, getting the residents of this neighborhood to care for babies and new mothers in such a Christian way. You are to be commended, of course. And so -- commending you is exactly what we plan to do, as one of the steps for the transition to a new directorship compliant with the holy precepts that are now the law."

As he paused, Rachel swallowed hard, before she responded:

"Magistrate, with all due respect…you mean to remove me from my position, where you point out I have been so effective – and to put some man in charge of this ministry center?! Some clergyman who does not have my background with what we do here? Or the people in-volved? HE cannot have the same success without the al-legiances and loyalties I have cultivated with blood, sweat, and tears – all because he has a 'Y' chromosome, and I do not?!"

Rachel was uncomfortably aware that her voice had risen. More than that, her face felt so flushed that it had to be some deep shade of red. And that very thought caused her to study the glint in Cromwell's eyes.

He spoke, as she peered into his eyes, in his calm, measured tones: "Rachel, as I pointed out earlier, this is not yet an official proceeding – not this morning, at any rate. So, please – let's continue without so much heat, shall we?"

As Rachel nodded, he continued: "Rachel, I can ap-preciate how distressing this must be for you. This min-istry is your baby: your prayers, your passion, your efforts have gone into this successful organization for years. And that clearly was the Will of the Lord Almighty. Now, it is painful to have me remind you that while you served as a midwife, and nanny, the actual parent of this baby is the Lord God. Now, it seems the Will of the Lord is for a change in leadership. At this time you are being asked to accept that the Lord is doing a 'New Thing.'"

As he said this last, the magistrate rose to stand, still fixing his gaze directly into Rachel's eyes, and his look was sympathetic. "And now, I think, I shall leave this informal conversation of ours, and leave you to some prayerful consideration about how best to face this change. Find some way to offer the most hope and strength to your organization. If you have any suggestions of a man for the job, let me know."

Rachel managed to make eye contact with him, and to gain her own feet, which she could no longer feel. She nodded mutely toward him. She neither saw nor heard the door open and close – she did not notice as Clarence paused with his hand on the doorknob – because her face had already bowed into her hands, as she collapsed into her chair. Her ears barely registered the second closing of the door, as she was overcome with a tsunami of shock and grief.

After some minutes, and several damp tissues, Rachel felt the need to telephone her husband, John. She needed to share her burdened heart with her best friend. Quickly she glanced at her watch, only to stare amazed at the realization that only half an hour had passed since her arrival at the center. With happy disbelief, Rachel realized she still had plenty of time to speak with John before his work shift began at nine o'clock.

She selected the button on her desk phone that would ring John's cell phone. He answered on the second ring, with his customary "Y'ello."

"Oh, John," Rachel half-gasped, half-sobbed. Instantly, his casual demeanor was gone.

"Sweetheart, what's the matter?!"

"He was here when I got here – the magistrate – in my office, waiting for me. And so we already met about the decree – though he said it wasn't yet official – he was clear about how things are going to be – and I was so stunned, so flustered that I didn't…"

The support in his warm voice reached out to her like a gentle embrace she could feel there in her office, where Cromwell's detached, immovable presence seemed to linger. "Rachel, honey -- I'm so sorry. But please slow down and breathe a little deeper, okay? Help me to understand, 'cause I thought the meeting wasn't until later this morning. And wasn't Martha going to be there with you?"

"Yeah, that's all true. But none of that is what's happening. First of all, Martha couldn't make it – she was called into court for the day. And, well…I don't know, John; my head is just whirling."

"Yeah, babe, I know. But at least it sounds like the leaking out from your eyes has mostly stopped." And that caused Rachel to smile. He knew her so well. That sly insertion of humor was so typical of her husband's way with her. And, it was one of the many things she adored about him.

"John, I love you. The thing is….My problem is, I don't know what I'm going to do! I don't have a clue what I can do about this!"

"I know, Rachel. And, I know you so well that I'm

pretty sure it doesn't occur to you that maybe you do nothing – because there truly is nothing anyone can do. Not even you."

"Huh?! No, you're right, my love, that does not occur to me. And if it were anyone else but you, Jonathan David DeLine, I would take offense at the very idea." Breathing a large sigh, and smiling again, she continued: "So, my dear, for your sake I'm going to overlook it, this time. Besides, I've got to let you get to work. And, I've just figured out what I can do next, and pretty much right away."

"Uh-huh," he replied, "and what, pray tell – 'your Reverendness' -- might that be?"

"Exactly that, sweetheart – I'll pray," she quipped. "So, I am off to the chapel. I love you, and I'll see you and Maggie at home after work. Bye."

After John's goodbye, Rachel disconnected. Then she got up and left her office to search for Clarence. After that, she would go to the chapel.

CHAPTER TWO

A teenage girl leaned against the brick wall of the light-rail station. Most of the small number of people who even knew the girl existed, called her by the nickname she had acquired growing up in an orphanage: "Lame." Her given name (given by an anonymous birth mother who dropped her off) was Bethany Marie Laham. The overpopulated orphanage had too many girls named "Beth" and "Betsy," so the staffers called them all by their surnames – in her case, Laham. But, it was the other orphans who began pronouncing it "lame," because they so frequently told her: "You're so lame!"

She wasn't really lame, in the physical sense, of course. But she frequently said and did things so unusual that the others could not ignore how she failed to fit in. Even in an orphanage, a typically female social mentality was prevalent among the girls, and Beth, with her wide gray eyes that seemed to see too much, and her lack of interest in the petty politics of a girl-group, had no safe place. She was just as unwanted among the boys, despite her slim, athletic frame and down-to-earth attitude – she was still a girl, and in that no-man's-land of early adolescence, she wasn't boyish enough to be accepted by the boys, and not willing to play the girls' game to be accepted by them, either. Her independence and refusal to play by unfair rules grew exponentially with every day that passed, as she watched and listened, quietly disapproving.

Beth wanted life to make sense – not necessarily to be fair, but to make sense, to have a framework she could understand; like the complex rules of chess, which she loved to play. Nobody at the orphanage would play with her, but occasionally she would go to the public library, where once a month they held a chess tournament, and she would play there – usually against a series of old men. She didn't mind; those old men seemed safe to her, because they were unfamiliar. They weren't like the kids who tortured her, or like the hard-edged matrons who ran the orphanage. Sometimes she looked across the board at these old men, with their lined paper-thin skin and dim eyes, and wondered if any of them could answer her questions -- the questions that disturbed the people at the orphanage. One of the biggest questions she had was why religion was presented in terms of sin and punishment, when Jesus had come to give a message of unconditional love. She didn't understand how the vengeful, wrathful God of the Old Testament could be the same God who sent his only son to be sacrificed for the world. And she didn't understand how a supposedly loving Father God could send his child to be murdered by a mob. When she asked these questions, she was disciplined. But she didn't care; she couldn't believe in these contradictions of Christianity, which were deeply offensive to her.

It was this failure to conform that led her, at the age of thirteen, to run away from the orphanage. When teenage peer-pressure intensified to an extreme level, she fled her captive torment. The trauma that catapulted her forth – from the only existence she had known – came when she refused to make unanimous the conversions to Christ of all the orphans residing there.

Thinking about it, she involuntarily put her hands over her ears for a moment, as if to shut out the memories of voices cajoling, wheedling, threatening…promising everlasting life – as if that were something anyone would want! – or telling her that if she did not accept Christ, she would go to hell. She was in hell at the orphanage, and couldn't imagine anything worse than that. She remembered the punishment she'd had to endure when she had said this: hours on her knees, scrubbing the toilets and the floors, her hands red and cracked from the bucket of disinfectant, her stomach clenched with hunger, for she was given only one meal a day for a week, in the hope that this would make her more cooperative. But a meal was not worth the price of her integrity, and she would not give in. On the last day of that week, her stomach tight with hunger, she had climbed down the fire escape from her third-story dormitory room, and ran away. For an hour or so she just ran, trying to get as far away as she could. She hadn't thought about where she would end up, or what she would do next. Finally, she found a park with some thick bushes, and she dropped behind them in exhaustion. When she awoke the next morning, she found several other teenagers, both boys and girls, asleep around her. She had been lucky, that night, rather than safe.

As time passed, she learned the sad, hard rhythm of the streets. She learned to sleep under picnic tables and in abandoned buildings. She checked doors and windows of empty houses, hoping to find a way in. Sometimes these places would still have running water, and she could enjoy the luxury of bathing and washing her clothes. She lurked around picnic areas and outdoor tables, sometimes stealing food when people's backs were turned. Other times, she looked through trash bins for discarded food. Her primary emotions were anger and fear. She had no friends; people used her, and she used them. It was all about survival, on the streets. She learned to be suspicious of others, and to mistrust herself. She was painfully aware that living on the streets had been her own choice, and she came to feel that she deserved the hardship that defined every day of her life.

Now, she was fifteen, living on the streets, belonging to no one, *and terrified*. It was not the homelessness that scared her -- Beth had adapted to life on the streets

-- dressing like a boy, keeping her hair short, and wearing baseball caps. What frightened "Lame" was her new physical loss.

Something was wrong with her. She'd quit having her monthly period. She didn't know just how long overdue she was, but it was many weeks, by now. And she had no one to ask, nobody to turn to for help. At first she had tried not to worry; her quick, adaptable brain had even seized on some of the advantages of not having a period – she didn't have to risk buying items at the store that gave her away as a girl. These items were expensive, and every month she dreaded trying to find the money, and worried about how long her supply would last. She worried about stray dogs on the street being attracted to the smell of blood; she worried about blood leaking through her pants, which would ruin her boy's disguise. Although her logical self recognized that not having a period had its advantages, she couldn't rationalize away the simple fact that her healthy body should be having one…and if it had stopped, it meant that her body was no longer functioning as it should. The flexible strength of her athletic young body was key to her safety on the streets. What would she do if she were ill, if something were seriously wrong with her?

As she moved quickly around the bulletin board on the train platform, to catch an illegal ride aboard the final car (hoping to go unnoticed by the ticket steward), her mind grappled with her predicament. Hunching over, and wedging herself between several preoccupied commuters, Beth could think only about how alone she was. This had never bothered her before, as solitude was better than any other option she had known in her young life. But now that she was in real need, maybe even serious trouble, she longed for a trusted someone in whom she could confide. She tried to imagine what it would be like to have a mother to talk to, but the thought was so alien that her mind had no frame of reference with which to even dream about such a thing.

Remaining slouched in the corner of the train car, in her boyish cap, jacket, and pants, Beth kept her face down, and her fingers took turns at her mouth, as she chewed her fingernails in nervous agitation. However, her inward focus was distracted by the voice of the woman next to her; it had a pinched, nasal quality, most obnoxious, and impossible to ignore.

"Why, thank you for asking! I am expecting – and six months along, now. My husband and I are so excited. We're even taking classes together, in the city, at the Early Steps Parenthood Center. Have you heard of them? Oh, they're good people there – and I've just 'locked-in' with the teacher – she's called Reverend Rachel. No, seriously – I mean it – I think she was like commissioned, or you know, some such...before, in the older days. 'Anywhoo', we're learning a lot, and let me tell ya, there's a lot to learn. I'm getting used to many new realities, lots of changes to myself, and to our lives. Yeah, that's the truth. But one change I don't mind is doing without the proverbial 'cotton bale' for a week each month, ya know what I mean?!"

As the realization hit her, Beth was so stunned that she almost failed to move with the flow of people getting off the train (to remain aboard for more than one stop was to risk getting caught). That woman had stopped having her period, too – as a part of pregnancy! So maybe there were reasons for her own to stop, other than the dread diseases she'd imagined!

Maybe, she thought, she could learn more at the same place the gal with the obnoxious voice had gone for advice and help. What had she called it? The center for parenthood – or, no – it was something about steps! First steps for parenthood center, or very close to that, Beth concluded. But one name she remembered for sure: a woman called "Reverend Rachel." Beth's memory of the forced conversions at the orphanage caused a flare of anxiety in her heart at the word "Reverend." But her choices were few, and her need was desperate. She would walk into this place under her own power, not as a ward in the legal custody of others, as she had been at the orphanage. If she didn't like what she found, she could walk right back out again.

Beth adjusted her cap, and set her delicate yet strong jaw in determination. In the downtown area of Colorado Springs, she might find an answer, and help. Another train going that direction would be along in eleven minutes.

———— ((◉)) ————

Rachel did not know just how long she had been in the silence of the chapel, lost in meditation and prayer. She had poured out her troubles to her Savior, and then reposed in a listening posture. She hoped for an answer in her mind or heart, or at least some peace – even deeper, within her spirit. Still, Rachel did not feel any more "answered" than when she had begun. She was neither surprised nor dismayed by this, for she knew what every mature believer understood: frequently, one's prayer vigils yielded no immediate, dramatic return on the investment. Just like the prayer itself, the responses were usually long-cultivated with patience and persistence. But there was still some comfort to be drawn simply from being in the chapel: jeweled light beamed down from the stained-glass window depicting Christ with His favorites, the innocent children, the vulnerable and tender souls to whom she herself felt most strongly drawn to protect. She closed her eyes again for a moment, not praying, but taking a silent moment in the quiet space, which smelled faintly of incense and of the old, solid wood of the pews, lustrous with the patina of many hands, many people who had prayed and sought peace here.

As she straightened herself, drawing a deep breath and preparing to take her leave of the sacred space, Rachel heard a small rustle of clothing from back near the doors to the chapel. Rachel turned around, and squinted through the alternating shafts of light and shadow to see the silhouette of the slight figure standing halfway in between the double doors of the chapel.

"Yes?" she asked. "Are you looking for me?" Her deep, rich voice echoed slightly in the chapel.

The figure moved another step inside the doors, yet still holding the door open, as if wanting to ensure an easy escape, should it be necessary. "I'm not sure, please excuse me – but I'm looking for Reverend Rachel – who works here." The voice, light and sweet as an angel's, belonged to a girl – though the figure looked boyish.

Rachel stood up and stepped into the aisle, as she said, "Well my dear, you found me. I'm the Rachel who works here." She slowly walked along the aisle toward the doors, and then she could see just how young her visitor was. "And since I was already finished with my prayers, I was just about to leave here anyway. You have not interrupted me, and I am available for you."

As Rachel drew closer to the girl, she could see how she trembled, her face pinched with worry. Rachel continued speaking: "It looks like you found me at just the right time -- for getting acquainted, I mean. How about we walk over here a few steps to my office, so you can tell me about how you found me, and what I can do for you."

Rachel rested her hand on the girl's slender shoulder,

as she asked the last question. The girl automatically flinched, but Rachel did not move her hand, allowing her kindness and goodwill to connect with the girl. After a moment, the girl relaxed. Looking more closely into that young face, Rachel saw such anxiety and loneliness that she was deeply touched. With all the compassion she felt, she smiled warmly at the girl, and then led her down the hall to her office.

As they entered, Rachel motioned to the girl to sit in one of the two nearby chairs. She noticed that the girl did not sit in the same chair Cromwell had chosen, and she wondered whether something of him lingered in the other chair…something forbidding, which this girl, so highly attuned to her surroundings, might somehow have felt. Rachel closed the door and turned back to her visitor. Rachel asked her, "Would you care for a mug of hot chocolate?"

As their eyes met, a look of relief crossed the girl's features, and she mutely nodded her acceptance of the offer. Rachel went over to her small counter. She took two plain white china mugs from the cupboard, and opened two packets of cocoa mix, filling the mugs with boiling water from the automatic hot-water tap in the sink. She stirred carefully to make sure the mixture was fully dissolved. After a moment of thought, she added a small handful of miniature marshmallows to the girl's mug. She usually kept the marshmallows for children, but something about this wayward young woman's expression told Rachel that she was, in many ways, a lost child, and that a special treat would disarm her a bit. She saw that she was right; when she handed the girl her mug, she looked at the melting marshmallows, and then back up at Rachel in pleased surprise. She did not smile, but her eyes twinkled just slightly, just enough to make Rachel glad she had thought to give a little extra. She sat down, not behind her desk, but next to the girl, in the other chair. She both wanted to erase Cromwell's energy from the room, and also to remove any barrier between herself and the girl – she didn't want the desk to be between them.

"What's your name?" Rachel asked.

The girl took a breath, then hesitated. She took a sip of her cocoa, and then tried again. "They call me 'Lame,' but my real name is Beth. I am an orphan, but I left the orphanage, a long time ago."

Rachel nodded sympathetically. "That bad, huh?"

"Yeah. For me anyway. I've never missed it."

"So you've been on your own for a while, I guess?"

"Ever since, yeah." Seeing the depth of compassion in Rachel's beautiful dark eyes, Beth shrugged, unsure whether it was safe to accept. "But it's not so bad," she said, her tone almost defensive – yet the sweetness of her voice lent a poignancy to her words. "I gotta keep my hair short, and wear guys' clothes – and a cap. But, I've hooked up with 'Friendlys,' and I've gotten by okay."

Rachel waited for a moment, a beat of respectful silence, before she said, "Beth, I'm amazed -- and impressed. You must be very strong, and very smart – and you've got me wondering what I could possibly do for you."

Looking away, the girl's face went through a series of expression changes, before she resumed eye contact with Rachel. She said, "Well, I'm having a problem. And I got this idea you might know about such things. I heard this woman talking, on the train…she's expecting a baby, and she said you helped her with her changes, you know. Now, I've got a big change in my body, too, and I don't know what's happening to me…and I'm not so strong or smart, see…and I'm just really scared, really…I just…I just didn't know of anything else to do…and I was hoping…"

The final words came out as a sob and then Beth was crying, and no more words could come out. Rachel stood and reached with both arms, and Beth quickly surged into the embrace, as sobs racked her slender body. As Rachel held the girl close, thoughts and feelings raced through her. In all her years as a care provider, never had she met anyone so solitary and tragic as this teenager. She wondered about Beth's life experiences, and marveled that the girl seemed so innocent and tender when most street urchins would have become jaded, and hardened with bitterness.

The girl even spoke of hope. Now, that was an amazing faith for someone whose entire, short life had been lived as an outcast! But Rachel knew what she needed to ask next, as Beth wound down from her emotional release, because she was pretty sure she knew what change in the girl's body was mystifying and terrifying Beth. She had seen countless women of all ages in this predicament; although she was accustomed to it, she never assumed how a woman would feel, or what had happened to her. Rachel's ministry was never routine; each woman, each child, was an individual, and she approached each story as if she had never heard it before. She gradually released Beth from the embrace, and indicated that they both should be seated, while handing her a box of tissues. And, when they were settled, Rachel asked her:

"Beth, you spoke of your body changing – could you tell me what you mean?"

"I suppose, yeah – I mean, that IS why I came here to find you. So, it's like this – about two months ago, I quit having my monthly bleeding period."

"I see. Beth, forgive me for asking such a question, but I must ask you…could you be pregnant?"

Beth's face was shocked. "Huh? Oh, NO! No, I couldn't be with child. I am not married – I've never gone to bed with a man! I've never even kissed a guy – NEVER!"

"Okay -- it's okay, Beth," Rachel soothed. "I just had to ask, you know, because that is the most common and typical reason for a woman's period to stop. I take it your period has always been regular, before this?"

"Yes, I think so…ever since it started – about a year before I left the orphanage."

Rachel nodded reassuringly. "Okay. Well, we have ways to check out what's going on. And don't worry -- we will help you. It is a good thing that you came to see me, Beth."

CHAPTER THREE

An hour later, Rachel was on the phone again, this time ringing the pager number for Martha McIntosh, her lawyer friend. The pager-alert had the effect she desired; five minutes later, her friend returned the call.

"Hey, Rachel. What's up?"

"Hi, Martha – thanks for responding so quickly. I know you've got your hands full, today – but, I've suddenly found mine overwhelmingly full, too. It looks like I need some legal advice."

"Oh, Rache, hon, I'm so sorry about missing that meeting this morning…"

Rachel interrupted her. "This is not about the magistrate, Martha! At least, not yet. This is another more urgent, probably more dangerous problem, dear. In fact, this is so confidential that I just realized I need to ask if you're alone."

"Not yet -- just give me a minute." Martha's tone betrayed no curiosity, to protect their privacy while she was still with people who could hear her. She had already spoken Rachel's name in the course of the conversation, so anyone overhearing them would have known whom she was speaking with. Rachel was grateful for Martha's immediate and reliable grace under pressure.

Rachel could hear muffled exchanges, footsteps, and doors opening and closing, then more footsteps. She bit her lip with the strain of waiting. She felt like she could sense the deep, sub-audible rumble of an avalanche beginning. Rachel was sure she was in the path of a suffocating danger.

"Rachel, I'm here, again! Tell me what's worrying you, hon."

"This is so difficult and dangerous, Martha – I've got a young, unmarried girl here, who is illegally pregnant! She's from the streets – a runaway orphan. Martha, she is adamant that she's never engaged in sexual intercourse… doesn't understand how she could be with child. And, well, I find her credible – even though that's an unbelievable story. It's just that she doesn't even seem to know the specific details of intercourse, and has only the vaguest idea of human reproduction. That's not so surprising, really, given what passes for 'female catechism,' these days. Honestly – they leave these kids so ignorant and naïve about human sexuality! I just gave her a pregnancy test, and I know she is pregnant…she was so confused about how that was possible; it was heartbreaking to see the look on her face. I know she believes me, and yet at the same time she doesn't see how it can be true. Anyway, she seems good and honest, and…"

Martha broke in, "Rache, wait a minute, okay? Let me see if I am getting this: the girl is underage and unmarried, and pregnant. Right? Yet, she claims she is not guilty of the misdemeanor crime of fornication?"

Hearing her friend speak the words aloud made Rachel realize how ridiculous her own belief in the girl must sound. "Yeah, I know, Martha. This is so crazy," she acknowledged. "But she's not what you'd expect – a runaway orphan, living on the streets – but, she's not jaded and cynical, you know. And…"

"Okay, my turn again, hon. So you like her, and you're disinclined to follow the dictates of holy law – to turn her in to authorities as required – because she is evidently a confused -- and nice -- criminal fornicator. Isn't that about right?"

Rachel ignored the irony in Martha's voice. "Oh yes, Martha – I just knew you'd understand…"

"Rachel, I do NOT understand. Okay? I comprehend, hon, but I cannot understand how you could be thinking of anything so dumb as shielding this girl from the Stewards of the Law! I mean really, Rachel! I love you like a sister, but…do you realize what such a move would make you? You would become a criminal accomplice!"

"Oh, dear God in heaven, Martha! I know!! I know this is insane…but, I just CAN'T do it! It feels so WRONG, with this girl, in this case. I mean…"

"Rache, listen to me: by sharing this with me, you've now ensnared me in the dilemma – *ex post facto* – and I'm at risk – as a possible accessory. Attorney-client privilege does not apply to the shielding of fugitives from justice!"

"Oh, Martha, I'm so sorry! I should have known better, I guess. I just couldn't think of anyone else to turn to – for advice, you know. And, I've got to help this girl. She makes me think of my own daughter! What can be done to save her from the black vans? I can't – won't betray her to that!"

"Well, love, since you've already decided against the only reasonable action – I must assume that you've drawn me into this quagmire to counsel you on some unreasonable courses of action to take. And that better be in person, not over the phone. Preferably someplace inconspicuous, and not until tomorrow… what if I meet you in the chapel, at the center, about mid-day…"

Rachel smiled to herself, relieved to have Martha's support, even though she knew Martha had good reason to be nervous. "Better make it after two. On Saturdays the place is vacant after we close at one o'clock."

"All right, Rachel. I'll be there. And I'll be looking scared, from the effort of making sure I haven't been noticed, or followed. Do you get me?"

"I do, my friend. And, thanks…thanks, Martha!"

"Okay, hon. Now be careful, and stay safe, until then. I'll see ya. Bye."

"Bye." And as she closed her phone, Rachel thought about taking Beth home with her. Then she thought about how sharing this with John would go. Finally, she thought she'd better be getting back to that unusual and pitiable girl waiting in her office.

⟢ ⟨◉⟩ ⟣

Rachel and Beth paused for a moment outside the soft grey bungalow-style duplex where Rachel's family lived. Since Beth was on foot, Rachel had walked her bike home; it took a little longer to get there, not using the bike paths, but she had enjoyed the extra time alone with Beth, who shyly shared a few small stories about life in the orphanage. Rachel listened actively, occasionally shaking her head in sorrow at the painful treatment Beth had endured. Beth watched Rachel as she wheeled her bike into the small bike alcove under the front stairs, and locked her bike to the rack on the wall.

"I don't really think anyone would steal it," she said, seeing the surprise on Beth's face. "It's habit, more than anything." Beth nodded, and pulled awkwardly at the bill of her cap. "Are you ready?" Rachel asked with a warm smile. Beth nodded, the small furrow of worry between her eyes contradicting her agreement.

Rachel unlocked and opened the door. She saw John and Maggie, their daughter, on the floor of the living room.

The five-year old girl was wearing her toy stethoscope, her hands groping around in her plastic medical bag. John was clearly the doctor's patient, with a toy thermometer stuck in his mouth. They both turned to look at Rachel, and then at Beth entering just behind her. Pleasure, and then confusion, appeared on both their faces.

"Hello, my loves," Rachel began. "I've brought a guest with me. Her name is Beth. We just became friends today -- and I'm sure you're going to enjoy getting to know her while we all have dinner together." She smiled at them and then at Beth in turn. Beth's eyes were wide as saucers as she looked around the room, taking in the comfortable beige-upholstered couch and easy chairs, the simple glass-topped tables and brass lamps, the family photos on the walls. Rachel realized that the girl had probably never been inside a house before.

"May I take your jacket and cap?" Rachel gently suggested, hanging her own jacket on the coat tree. Beth reluctantly surrendered both. Rachel saw that underneath the jacket, she was wearing only a thin, short-sleeved black t-shirt. Her glossy brown hair, cut in a blunt jawline-length bob, looked less boyish without the hat. To smooth over the shy awkward glances exchanged between family and guest, Rachel continued: "Speaking of dinner, John, how's it coming?"

Handing the thermometer to Maggie and struggling to his feet, John replied, "Things should be all ready when the six o'clock news is over." Then moving across the room toward the women, he said, "Say, you just barely made it home in time. Another five minutes and curfew would have caught you, until after seven!" Reaching out to Rachel, he kissed her and said, "I'm glad you're home." Then turning to Beth, he added: "Beth, welcome to our home. I look forward to getting acquainted." Beth ducked her head shyly, and did not offer her hand. He smiled and said, "You know what – it's chilly tonight. Rachel, I think Beth might like to borrow that red wool cardigan of yours."

By this time Maggie had made her way over to them, and opened her arms to indicate that her mommy should pick her up. So, Rachel did – kissing and hugging her, as well. John chuckled. "I'll go get the cardigan," he said. Rachel smiled gratefully at him. When Maggie's eyes shifted to the stranger, Rachel spoke to her daughter. "Mag, I'd like you to meet Beth; she's nice. Beth, this is my special little girl, my Maggie."

Beth forced a small smile to Maggie and said, "Hello, Mag."

Maggie, wide-eyed, said nothing. John came back into the room, carrying a long-sleeved sweater in a rich shade of red. Gallantly, he held it up for Beth, who cautiously slid her arms into it after looking over at Rachel for permission. As soon as she felt the warm soft wool against her skin, she drew the sweater close around her, snuggling up in it, an almost dazed look on her face. Rachel's heart contracted painfully again with the knowledge of how starved this child was for love, for simple care.

John looked at his watch, and indicated (exchanging glances with Rachel) that it was time to move over to the sofa and chairs for the required viewing of the video newscast. Rachel, John, and Maggie sat together on the sofa, while Beth claimed her own private space in one of the chairs, drawing her legs up underneath her, settling down into the folds of the cardigan.

The view-screen on the opposite wall was filled with animated shapes and colors, generating a celestial appearance. Music from a choir swelled to a crescendo on the refrain of the hymn "A Mighty Fortress Is Our God." As the music faded, the CGI visuals gave way to an emerging scene: a good-looking man stood facing his audience, wearing a friendly look on his face. His eyes sparkled as he began to speak.

"Good evening, faithful folks. Tonight, the church wants you to know that our godly nation is safe, as we continue shining like a beacon for the rest of this dark and troubled world. I am Gordon Whitfield, your herald of good news on this blessed evening. And I bring you several reports of the triumphal marching of the Lord, also a celebration of thanksgiving, and one minor update – for the good of our social order. So, let me proceed with today's victories for Christ and the Heavenly Father."

On the view-screen, the scene shifted to an aerial view of a large city, dotted here and there with flaming buildings, its air filled with dark and moving clouds of smoke. The camera's vantage point showed the bright flashes of weapons being fired. Then the camera zoomed in toward the obvious battle raging along a river, as the herald's voice continued:

"Here, you can observe how our 'Joshua Forces' fulfill their God-given patriotic duty, by securing our borders. These views show the battle in and around the largest city of 'Nineveh,' formerly known as Detroit, on the banks of Lake Erie." Softly the music began; it was the "Battle Hymn of the Republic." "You'll recall that this is where most of the Islamic infidels fled during the Transition Time. They organized themselves into an insurrection, and mounted their rebellion against the holy will of God. Their resistance continues only because they receive aid from some Middle-Eastern governments. Yet we know their insurgency will fail, for Christ the Lord is on our side!"

The music rose to a climactic finale. Then Whitfield said, "Let us pause for a moment of grateful, silent prayer." After seven seconds of silence, the herald (and the music) began again:

"Our sacred vigilance continues within, as well as beyond, our borders. Today, near the former University of Pennsylvania, Law Stewards raided a house where dozens of Quakers were secretly hiding. Seen here, these are the heretics who were arrested, and loaded into God's chariots. They will be transported to immediate and permanent exile on Judas Island. Yes, Christ's truth is marching on, and this nation's purification continues. There have been no more deportations of Jews for many months, nor any Unitarian blasphemers arrested for well over a year! But be assured, gentle spirits, one day soon we will fully be the pure and devout Christian nation of our manifest destiny!"

Beth shifted uncomfortably in the chair, and huddled down further into Rachel's sweater. She wondered what Rachel would think if Beth told her she had refused to convert at the orphanage – that she had fled that place, rather than conform. The scene shifted once again, as did the musical score. "In a more peaceable, yet also victorious report, the 'Natural Law of Adam and Eve' was obeyed and celebrated, this very day. Hundreds of reclaimed souls, formerly enslaved to abomination, were joyously engaged in holy matrimony, as man and wife – the way God intended. They were united in this blessing of normal life and natural love before 100,000 witnesses at the Coliseum of Roses, in Pasadena.

"And now, God's beloved citizens, a word of instruction regarding your virtuous obedience to the authorities that Christ has set over us all, for peaceful order. The gender-specific dress code will now be enforced by the law stewards. Please note that the penalty for transgressions by either gender will include public shaming. So please, sisters and brothers, be clothed in righteousness – as the Good Book says."

And with that witty remark, The Herald's handsome face broke into full smiling radiance.

Beth looked obliquely at her jacket and cap hanging on the coat tree. Things had always been hard for her...but she could tell they were about to be even harder.

"This is Gordon Whitfield, on behalf of the holy governance shepherding this Christian nation, wishing you a blessed night of safety and peace."

"Well," John began, as he clicked off the view-screen, "how about we move to the table for another peace – a piece of chicken that is!" And he grinned, chuckling softly at his own wit and humor. Rachel gave a sisterly smile of chagrin toward Beth, complete with rolling her eyes. Maggie whooped a "yippee!" exclamation, racing her dad to the table. Beth was shy and slow in joining them – she had never been close to such behavior before – and she was uncertain of the mood and the spirit of this little family. Surreptitiously, she placed the palm of her hand against her belly. A child was growing there...a child who might be a beautiful little girl, like Maggie. Would she be a good mother, like Rachel was? She hoped Rachel could teach her. She didn't know anything about how to be a parent. She was still barely out of childhood herself – a childhood in which she had been unwanted, outcast, and alone.

These three people seemed so easy, casual, and warm with each other -- even with her! This was like stepping into a completely different world for Beth. Never having known the security of belonging to anyone, and never having had anyplace to call home, she was overwhelmed by the graceful and familiar manner of this little circle of affection. They passed food around the table, eating with enjoyment and gratitude. Beth could not remember the last time her stomach had felt full, but now she was encouraged to eat as much as she liked of the pan-fried chicken, boiled potatoes, and crisp green salad. There was a simple and short table-prayer led by Maggie, and a concluding ritual by candlelight (recounting for one another the summation of their daytime experience). Beth became enchanted, deeply touched by the amazing meal. Until, that is, the time came for her, in turn, to open up and share her day with the others.

"Well, umh, this day was different from all the others in my life. I've met the three of you – starting with Rachel – and you are such n-nice p-p-people…" was all she managed, as her tears surprised her. Then the sobs overtook her, and she began to break into all-out bawling. Rachel moved to her side with a gentle embrace, once again. Quietly, John and Maggie moved with the dishes, around the corner into the little kitchen, and gave the two women some sacred space.

———(((●)))———

Later, after making Beth a place to sleep on the floor of Maggie's room, Rachel and John lay down together in bed. He began their "pillow talk" with: "She seems like a nice girl, that Beth. So, where did you collect her? And what's behind this emotional sleep-over?"

Rachel looked deeply into his hazel eyes, and touched his cheek, as she said, "You know how I was upset over losing directorship of the center? Well, I did go into the chapel to pray, after we talked on the phone. And when I was through with prayer – that is when Beth came in – into the center, to see me. In fact, she found me while I was still in the chapel – that is where God brought us together. And, well, she came looking expressly for me, having heard about me – by reputation – on some transit train. Oh John, she really found me – she's found the very heart of me! She is this innocent child, who's never belonged to anyone, never been loved by anyone – and now, she is going to have a baby!"

"Wait a minute -- she's pregnant?!" When Rachel affirmed this with her eyes, he continued: "But, Rachel, we know what causes that! You say she's never been loved by anyone? Well, somebody did some physical loving. Or, maybe she was drugged and raped?"

"No, she says not. And, as absurd as it sounds, she says

she has never even been kissed, even though her pregnancy test was positive. And, John – she appears to me to be genuinely honest when she tells me this."

"Huh? My next thought was to suggest maybe she was duped and drugged, so she doesn't remember being raped – but, well…"

"My love, I find this girl not only believable, but so very likable. Thinking of her life experience to this point, my heart aches for the love she has never known, and I'm amazed she isn't hard, bitter, and caustic like other street urchins I've met. I just don't know what to do with this – how to help her, you know…"

"Rachel," he interrupted, and now his gaze was quite intense. "Hon, you realize what we're into here? This is serious trouble…this is not something for us to resolve… Rachel, this is a matter of LAW! It's for the law stewards to deal with!"

"But, John – do you think she deserves to be hauled away in one of those black vans, and never seen, nor heard from, ever again?!"

"I don't judge. It's like…like I said to you earlier: there are certain things you cannot do anything about. In this case, the only thing to do is to contact the authorities, and turn Beth, and her dilemma, over to them."

"That's what Martha said, too. Although…"

"Wait. You already shared this with Martha – and received legal advice?! Then why are you trying to risk serious trouble?!"

"John – you say you don't judge, but you sound judg-mental to my ears. This became a forced choice, a 'judg-ment call'- from the moment Beth told me her problem. I AM forced to decide – to judge what my conscience can stand to live with for the rest of my days! If I do the safe thing, and turn her in, then I am merely the first judge of several who will determine her fate! And maybe the oth-ers will be just as self-serving!"

"And if you risk everything to avoid doing what the law requires?"

"I don't know, John. And because I am so unsure – that is why I am seeking more time for my head and heart to – to – you know, get together. And, that's all I can tell you, right now. Maybe tomorrow will offer wisdom?"

"What's tomorrow?" John wondered.

"I'm meeting with Martha in person. She was at the courthouse when I called her, and we couldn't talk safely. She is going to meet me at the chapel tomorrow."

John was reassured by this. Martha was highly ca-pable, highly intelligent, and would look out for Rachel's best interests. Underneath Martha's proper, controlled ex-terior there lay the heart of a warrior, and he knew she loved Rachel dearly. "Yeah. Okay, hon. You know, I love you."

"And I love you, too – my soul-mate. Good night."

As Rachel turned off the bedside lamp and rolled over

so her husband could snuggle up to her, she gave thought to a last little prayer for the days ahead:

"Give me courage to do what I can, acceptance of what I cannot, and most of all – the wisdom to know the difference."

CHAPTER FOUR

The following morning was Saturday, and the start to the day at the DeLine household was casual and gradual. By the time Beth awoke from her deep sleep of the exhausted, the other three had long since eaten and begun their individual activities for the morning. For a disoriented moment, Beth wondered where she was. Even the floor of the Mag's bedroom was more comfort than she'd had since she started living on the streets. She was still wearing Rachel's sweater, and seeing it brought back memories of the night before. She could still hardly believe how welcoming and kind the DeLines had been.

Beth got up, wondering vaguely what time it was. She came out of the bedroom and saw Mag quietly playing with a large pile of snap-together building blocks. Mag looked up as Beth, yawning and rubbing her head, looked around for the others.

"Mom has gone to the center for a while, and Dad is in there," Mag said, pointing to a small room on the opposite side of the living area. "He's busy *fiddling with* some of his work," she continued. She spoke the words "fiddling with" carefully, obviously quoting her father, not entirely sure what fiddling with some work might be. "We ate already – but I can show you the food." She gazed innocently up at Beth with soulful dark eyes like her mother's.

Beth just nodded her head and muttered, "Thanks." She wandered into the kitchen and saw a plate of pancakes covered with plastic cling wrap, and another covered plate with crisp bacon. Beth looked at the stove and oven, but she had no experience with kitchens, and she was afraid to use them, fearing that she might do something wrong. John and Rachel had been so kind to her already; she didn't want to disturb John and ask him to heat her food for her. She made a sandwich of cold pancakes and bacon, and was not surprised that everything at the DeLines' was wonderful...even the cold leftovers.

⸻ ⟪◉⟫ ⸻

It was Saturday morning at Angelica Fowler's, as well. She and her husband, Kirk, had been living in the other half of the DeLines' duplex since they moved in as newlyweds, six years before. The Fowlers were "True Believers" of Christian America, and devoted volunteers for the manifest mission of the national church, committed to purifying and ordering its utopian theocracy. So, in addition to working as an accountant for a large grocery chain, Angelica served her Lord as a commissioned

"Parish Monitor." This meant she was responsible for observing her neighbors, and keeping alert for any violations of holy precepts and sacred discipline. Upon discovering any form of disobedience by her neighbors, she was responsible to secretly report her observations to the city magistrate. Angelica thrived on correct performance of her duties, whether in her marriage, her occupation, or her holy servant's role; she yearned for perfection, and the assurance that she was well within the behavioral compliance that would reward her with an eternity in heaven.

So when she heard a new, unfamiliar, young voice speaking with Mag on the DeLines' patio that morning, Angelica was compelled to give the voices much closer inspection. She discreetly maneuvered herself, with a cup of tea and her Bible, to one of the chairs on her own patio, to eavesdrop. Even though it was Saturday, she was nicely dressed in a gray twill skirt and white blouse, her fair hair pulled back into a tight bun. She sat in her patio chair with her back straight, knees and ankles carefully pressed together, her head cocked slightly to one side with the effort of eavesdropping.

Next door, because it was a sunny and mild day, Mag sat outside petting a grey tabby cat, who was sunbathing on the DeLines' patio. After Beth had eaten, she wandered out to join them on the patio. The cat was purring loudly, as the young girl's small hands rubbed its cheeks and neck.

"This is Esmeralda. I named her for the girl in that movie – The Hunchback of Notre Dame. You know, the one who makes friends with the hunchback."

Squatting down next to them, Beth looked at the cat, and said, "Hello, Esmeralda. You're very lucky to live here with this family." She thought about the thin, wary stray cats she usually saw on the streets. This soft, happy cat was as unlike those poor homeless pets as she was unlike the DeLines.

"Yeah. She mostly sleeps on my bed at night. But she didn't last night."

"Probably because I was sleeping in your room."

"Yeah. But, she's not scared of you anymore! Lookie!" The cat sat up and rubbed her face against Beth's hand, purring loudly.

"Wow, she's very friendly."

"She likes you."

Beth tentatively ran her hand over the glossy striped fur, while the cat continued her booming purr. Maggie beamed, happy that everyone was getting along so well. "I guess she does. Well, Esmeralda – I'm flattered. You're just like the rest of your family – very nice, I mean."

"We think you're nice, too."

"You don't think I'm lame?"

"Ummh – like with a broken leg?"

"No. I mean like weird, or goofy."

"No." The simple assurance of Maggie's reply tugged

at Beth's heart.

"Well, most people have called me 'lame,'" Beth blurted out, feeling that it was safe to share a bit of her hurt. "Like it was my nickname, you know? 'Cause they thought I was pretty strange."

"I like calling you Beth. That's your real name, isn't it?"

"Well, yeah. But, my full name is Bethany Marie Laham."

"Oh, yeah – I got a long name, too! Mine is Mary Margaret DeLine."

"Except you like to be called just 'Mag,' right?"

"Or Maggie. I don't really like Margaret…I wish my long name was Mary Mag DeLine!"

Next door, Angelica gasped as she took a drink of tea, and wound up choking.

There was a pause between the two girls, as they smiled shyly at each other. Mag resumed petting Esmeralda, pulling her into her lap. Beth was quiet, with a faraway look on her face. Then Mag spoke again.

"Esmeralda knows good people to like."

With a look of surprise, Beth replied: "Thank you, Mag. You're so nice – just like your mom."

"Yeah. Mommy makes lots of friends, helping lots of people, and so lots and lots of people know her. Is she helping you, too?"

Suddenly uncomfortable, Beth struggled with her reply. On the patio next door, the Parish Monitor had quit both the tea and her Bible, sitting still and attentively listening. After a moment's hesitation, Beth said,"Well, yes. As much as anybody can, anyway. I know she's trying to help me, Mag. It's just that…well, I don't know how to explain…but it's complicated."

"Oh. Umh, 'complicated' means it's too grown-up for a little kid like me, I know. Isn't that so?"

"Mag, you sure are smart!"

"So, is it about babies? I mean, I know that's what Mommy mostly helps ladies with."

Suddenly, Beth was uneasy, as her "street-sense" jolted her gut with a feeling of danger. She looked around at the small patio area, enclosed by the five-foot-high "privacy fence," and she felt exposed. So she looked Mag in the eyes and said, "Let's go inside, and I'll try to tell you what I can, Mag." Maggie simply nodded and picked up Esmeralda, holding her to her chest as they both stood up and went through the patio door.

On the other side of the fence, Angelina gathered her cup and her Bible, and left her patio. She went to get her phone, to call this in.

———⋘◉⋙———

Martha McIntosh made her way to the Early Steps center, steering her four-door hydro-car through the streets of Colorado Springs with no traffic delays, as it

was Saturday. Martha felt overwhelmed with trouble –
the trouble that had engulfed her. Here she was, an officer
of the justice system, and yet, because she loved her friend
Rachel, Martha was neglecting her duty for the first time
in her career. She could not avoid dwelling on the crisis,
and the consequences of the choices she and Rachel were
making. Her husband Jacob had earnestly questioned her
departure to meet with Rachel at the center on a Saturday.
He wanted Martha with him, of course, on a day that was
usually spent together. When he had said this, Martha
had a feeling that he wanted to spend time with her
because that was the correct thing to do on a Saturday,
rather than because he really wanted her company. It was
hard for her to gauge his actual feelings; his stolid, large-
featured face rarely betrayed any emotion. He'd suggested
that telephones had a divinely inspired purpose for speaking with friends on Saturdays, without leaving home. This
only intensified, within Martha, the certainty she felt that
this breach of legal obligation could only spell disaster for
her, and for her friend. But her love for Rachel would not
allow her to break her promise to meet at the chapel.

Nothing about this meeting was easy. Under the new
government, cars were rare; because they were hydrogen-
powered, they were extremely expensive to build, especially since the West Coast, where they were developed,
had seceded from the rest of the United States, making
it necessary to reverse engineer the technology. Certain

types of professions were given government grants to buy cars; lawyers were among those who received a vehicle subsidy, because they were expected to help clients get to and from meetings, and to be on time for court dates, etc. In exchange for the vehicle subsidy, Martha had to spend no fewer than five hours every week using her car for charity transportation, helping people who were too old, ill, or injured to easily use a bicycle or public transport. It was highly suspicious for Martha to be alone in her car on a Saturday, when she would not have business to attend to. If she had been driving toward her home, she could have said she had just completed a charity transport. But clearly, she was driving away from home. She fretted over whether she should have come by bicycle, but she had to be home in time to have dinner with Jacob and their friends, the Walkers, and since she had no idea how long the meeting with Rachel would take, she couldn't risk being late getting back home. The fifteen-minute drive from her house to the Center took an hour by bike.

Because she felt like a criminal accomplice, Martha passed by the center and gave only a furtive glance at the parking lot, while she headed her vehicle for a parking stall on the street, one block away. The lot was empty. So, after parking her car, Martha walked the sidewalk back to the center, trying to scan for witnesses without looking guilty! "Oh, Rachel," she thought, "If only you weren't the sweetest, most caring person I've ever known! I really could have done without all of this!"

Meanwhile, Rachel was inside the chapel of the center, engaged in fervent dialogue with God – however one-sided it seemed. Having walked all over the inside of the building, and verified that she alone remained, Rachel felt compelled to await her friend's arrival in the place where this crisis had begun. She could never explain to another soul how "non-coincidental" it all seemed to her; nor about her perception that this was a divine matter. It had been God who led the orphan girl to find her – a "God-incident" rather than a random accident. Such occurrences were familiar in Rachel's experience – though she had never before experienced one of such impact, and such potential jeopardy. It was not from an overblown ego, nor some distorted sense of self-importance, that she perceived the weightiness of this crisis; it was from her abundant experience with ordinary crises that she recognized this difference. Her perception was also the result of more than thirty years spent in daily communion with the living spirit of holiness. The depth of awareness this provided her could not mistake the fingerprints of the divine all over this chaotic mess. Rachel sighed with devout realization, and acceptance, that mere mortals cannot comprehend the inscrutable ways of this world's sacred creator, redeemer, and sustainer. She thought of the mantra: "Ours is not to reason why, but only to faithfully live and die." So, she would faithfully protect the innocent, come what may.

———•((•))•———

Across the city, in the palatial offices of the magistrate, Jerry Cromwell was also concerned with innocence. He was poring through the compiled reports of all the Parish Monitors for Colorado Springs. Before dispensing the information to the assorted tribunals for their assessment and investigation, Cromwell liked to view the collective picture of the impurities afflicting his parish. He did this on Saturdays, so he could refine certain emphases in his Sunday morning preaching of the Holy Lord's message. He knew that although an understanding of Christ's mind was beyond most sinful mortals, quite the opposite was true for such as he -- those who had been ordained to read the tell-tale indications in the world, using the light of God's infallible Word in the Bible. His responsibility, and challenge, was to analyze the eddying and pooling of sin, as it washed upon portions of his community with its eroding nature. And then, he must point it out – with the bright spotlight of the Lord's Truth – so it could be eradicated.

On this Saturday, he was dutifully performing this discipline, when his dedicated "hotline" telephone rang on the desk beside him. This was so unusual that he thought it must be a mistake, and he waited for a second full ring before he pushed the button to activate reception on the small view-screen. Only forty people in his parish had this secret phone number, so he was familiar with the woman's face on the screen: Angelina Fowler, a Parish Monitor. She waited for him to speak.

"Angelina, you are reporting a serious breach of holy ordinance?" he asked, his smooth, elegant voice making this query sound strangely welcoming.

"Yes, of course, Magistrate. Otherwise, I would not bother you."

He nodded. "Report, then, 'eyes and ears of the Lord.'"

Angelina composed her manner, her features, and her voice in the proper way she had been trained (this was important, to avoid the sin of gossip, but also to show pious respect for both her function and that of the magistrate – so that Christ the Lord would be pleased with their service). She reported all that she had seen and heard at the DeLines' residence that morning, and left dangling all the implications. With his knowledge and wisdom, the magistrate would consider the ramifications. He would ask the appropriate questions where he desired more thoughtful reflection on her part. Her sublime duty was fulfilled by speaking only when required of her.

When Angelina had finished reporting, Magistrate Cromwell did have one question for her: "Have you observed any other visitors to the DeLines' home on this day – or any departures by Mr. or Mrs. DeLine?"

Angelina carefully scaled back the eagerness in her

voice. "Sir, no one has come to their door, and the only one to leave was Rachel -- on her bicycle. She usually goes to the center on Saturday mornings."

"And has she returned?"

"No sir, not yet. And, that is unusual – since it is now more than an hour after they close for the day. She is usually home about an hour after."

"I see. Thank you, Angelina. You were right to bring this to me. You have served the Lord God with this, I am quite sure. Peace be with you."

With those words of dismissal, Cromwell immediately pushed the button on his phone, terminating the connection. His mind had already begun its rapid thinking: formulating postulates of logical calculation around the minimal details he'd received. None of these calculations entailed anything except a probable intrusion of serious sin into the DeLine family, and thereby into the larger community, whose purity was his responsibility as magistrate. He would have to protect the whole body of Christ's devout society, just as a physician would isolate and eliminate threats to an individual organism. This meditation was the first step; then after some time in prayer, he would consult the Quorum of Elders via cyber-conference, before organizing the response of his Colorado Springs servants.

CHAPTER FIVE

When Rachel finally returned home, it was less than an hour before the curfew of the evening news. Wearily climbing off her bicycle, and stowing it in the bike alcove, were mindless exercises in habitual motion. She had never before felt this haggard and world-weary. Never in her imagination had she thought such turmoil and emptiness could grip her soul. Only the bedrock convictions of her faith – believing in the supreme value of compassion, and the ultimate, eventual triumph of divine virtues – kept her sane and functional. Rachel was suffering too much sudden loss. Her entire life had been blown away like a tumbleweed before a tornado, simply because Beth Laham came to her for help. In her sacred commitment to kindness, and to protecting God's innocent ones, Rachel was now out of options – only one possible path lay open before her. The afternoon discussion and debate with Martha, a Biblical wrestling with one of God's angels, brought home a painful revelation! The facts of this situation had hammered and forged one inescapable realization: she and Beth had to flee the country, within hours!

Her steps were labored as she climbed the stairs. Her tight, shallow breathing came not from the physical exertion, but from the anxiety of facing John with the results of her afternoon. How hard this would be for all of them! Oh, Lord! She still struggled to accept the sudden conversion of her total existence – the overwhelming flood of danger and urgency that was sweeping her far from home, and inevitably "out to sea." Yet it was not only Rachel who was caught up in this; it also involved her husband and daughter. Oh, Maggie! "How can I keep you safe – without letting go of Beth, who will be washed away and drowned, if I do? Should I dare hazard you, my precious child, as I try to save another?" These thoughts brought her tears.

And then, even as her thoughts of Maggie took form, Rachel was looking into her daughter's face – through the glass of the storm door. The girl had been keeping a lookout for her, with the front door already open and… Rachel struggled for emotional stability as she looked into Maggie's eyes. Then the door was open, and she was hugging her little sweetheart, with a desperate urgency that puzzled the child.

"Mommy?! Are you okay, Mommy? We thought you were lost!"

"Oh, honey…I'm sorry to make you worry. But I'm here now, and everything is…we're just fine, now. Right?

Okay, then. Let's get me inside, shall we? There we go. Where's your daddy?"

As if on cue, John emerged from the hallway into the front room, to greet Rachel with a slightly cautious smile, and said, "Hello, prodigal. We were just about to put out the 'missing person alert.'" His eyes were studying her with barely concealed concern. Again, Rachel found herself struggling inside for an emotional equilibrium that she did not feel. Her loved ones needed (and deserved) all her strength to provide some ballast for the arriving storm. So, Rachel mustered a smile, and said, "I'm sorry to be gone so long. But Martha and I found that we had so much to talk about. And, well, we just kept talking and talking, you know. And then -- WOW! Is it really almost 5:30?" As John nodded his head, she continued, "I guess… well, it's almost time for the news – I guess I've messed up dinner, huh?" John continued to watch her, his expression halfway between concern and wariness. This disfluency and confusion were unlike her. He knew there was something wrong, and he also knew she couldn't tell him just yet. He desperately wanted to ask, but held himself in check. "Where is our guest?" Rachel asked. Just then, also as if on cue, Beth emerged from the kitchen holding a bowl and wearing an apron, and shyly smiling. John spoke before either woman could.

"As you can see, we didn't wait for your help with dinner. Beth asked if I could teach her how to help me, and

I have to say, I've never seen such a quick learner." Beth ducked her head shyly in response to John's warm smile. Rachel saw that the girl's guileless charm tugged at his heart, too. Knowing that would make her news easier to tell him…but it still wouldn't be easy.

"I helped, too!" Mag chimed in.

"Great," Rachel said, with genuine relief and gratitude. Then, turning to face John, she said, in a different tone: "John, could you follow me to the bedroom for a couple of minutes? Girls, thanks for taking care of the meal. We'll all sit down for the newscast in just a little bit." And with that, she turned down the hallway, concentrating hard to keep from stumbling, as the burden of the moment nearly staggered her. Take up your cross and follow Me, she thought. She had never more clearly understood those words spoken by Jesus. John turned to follow her, while pondering the obvious effort involved in Rachel's performance of a false "normality." He thought of the day Rachel told him they were expectant parents – because both the similarities to and the discrepancies between this "mysterious Rachel with the news" were phenomenal, and disorienting to him. Back then she had seemed joyfully sly – but, now she seemed burdened, and distant, almost like someone he did not know.

As they entered the bedroom, and Rachel closed the door, he studied her face closely while reaching for her hands to draw her close to him. Then, face-to-face, holding hands and looking deeply into each other's eyes – just as they had done at their wedding, exchanging vows – this newest moment of destiny was breached.

"John," she began.

"Rachel," he interrupted. "You're scaring me!"

"My love," she continued. "I'm scared, too! I don't know how to...I mean, if there were any other way...I, uhm...oh, John," and then Rachel's voice failed, as an uncontrollable shaking took hold of her entire body.

And then John became truly terrified, and needed them to sit on the edge of their bed. As he guided the shaking Rachel to sit, John swallowed hard, and said, "Rachel, I know we're facing a difficult choice here, but..."

"John," she interrupted, "if only there were any choice – but really, there isn't – I cannot abandon Beth – give her over to the law stewards, as if she were some criminal. So, there is – honestly – only one thing to do." Her shaking intensified, as she continued, "We have to – Beth and I have to flee from the law. I have to run away from home, and take her with me. It became clear as Martha and I talked, today – this is the only other option!"

The look on his face said everything he could not speak to her. The astonishment and the shock; the struggle to believe what he had just heard – it was all painfully etched upon his face. He frowned with concentration, as he endeavored to comprehend this unbelievable turn of fate. His gaze went far distant, and then came back to look into her eyes, bewildered. "Rachel?" it came out as a question. "Tell me this cannot be happening – I...I, uh... you..." he stammered, as words began to fail him, once again.

Rachel's eyes flooded with tears, as she felt the pain of her lover. Then, she collapsed into him, clutching both his shoulders with desperation, her cheek against his, as her shaking turned into convulsive sobbing. With the reflexive embrace of love, he clutched his wife to his chest – where the pounding of two faithful hearts became as close as physically possible. Again, he tried for words:

"Where would you go? How...? What about Maggie and me?!"

"I'm not sure. I don't know, John. We've got to figure this out. All I am certain of is this: Beth and I are *already* fugitives from the law, and we *have to run*, and maybe we will have to keep on running."

Taking hold of her shoulders, he held her out from him enough that he could look deeply into her eyes, and said, "You know my love for you, sweetheart – but this seems so crazy – maybe I've gone insane, or maybe it is you who have done so! But Rachel – how can this be?! What is happening here?"

With a somber, somewhat haunted look at him, she said, "I am afraid you married a devoted disciple of Christ Jesus, my love. And it seems that it's our time to answer the challenge of the cross – to lay down our lives for the sake of saving someone else. All I can be sure of is this: although I love you and Maggie more than life itself, there is no one else who can save Beth, except me…and you. It's like this has been thrust upon us… and there is only us." She tried to smile for him, but it came off as a grimace. "We must not fail now, my love."

<hr>

Several minutes later, Rachel and John were gathered in the living room with Mag and Beth, to view the evening newscast, as required. Neither John nor Rachel gave much heed to the herald on the screen, nor to the reports of the day's victories in the name of triumphal Christ. In fact, they were so inwardly focused with their fear and anxiety that it took an audible gasp from Beth to turn their attention toward the video. Rachel uttered a "What?" as the both looked to the view-screen with renewed alertness, then dismay!

The voice of the herald was speaking over a scene so unusual and so disturbing that the words "CHILD ALERT" were flashing in red animation near the bottom of the screen. The herald said: "Viewers with children in the room are required at this time to dismiss the children for this final report of tonight's newscast." John reacted quickly, ushering Mag from the room.

The image on the view-screen, frozen in still-picture,

was that of a dozen men who were naked above the waist, all chained together by both handcuffs and leg shackles, being led out of the back of a black van by several Law Stewards. Their only covering was something like a wrap-around skirt. Their heads had all been shaved, and they seemed to have marks on their foreheads.

After a thirty-second pause, the alert caption disappeared, and the video resumed action. The camera zoomed in on the faces of the prisoners as they shuffled toward the large institutional-looking building. Their faces all shared the glassy-eyed stare of horror with which most condemned met their demise. As John rejoined Beth and Rachel, the voice of the herald spoke over the vision of a dozen terrified men:

"These despicable sinners are some of the worst to infect and to afflict our civilized society. They are the sexual miscreants, perverts, and predators who have been shaming and disgracing our communities with sins too hideous and atrocious to further elaborate. You will note that upon their foreheads has been branded the letter of their abomination – 'A' for adulterers, 'R' for rapists, 'P' for perverted pedophiles, and 'S' for sodomites.

"Each of these convicted repeat felons will be neutered, according to the law for such crimes. Then, after their prescribed periods of penitence and careful reprogramming, all of the survivors will be returned safely to our peaceful society. The permanent letter branded upon their foreheads, however, will allow them, and the rest of us, to remember the redemption of their past."

Suddenly the DeLines' attention to the riveting horror of the newscast was disrupted by the sound of retching, as Beth, overcome by pregnancy and by terror at what she had just seen, vomited onto the floor and then fainted.

———⟨⟨◍⟩⟩———

At the McIntosh home, Rachel's best friend Martha, with her husband Jacob, had finished sharing dinner with their friends and neighbors – Susan and Rob Walker. As Martha set the last of the cleared dishes in the sink, Jacob got out the group's favorite word-scramble board game. Their home phone suddenly rang. Martha closed the front door and looked over at Jacob. It was uncommon to receive a phone call at home on a Saturday evening. Of course, Martha's cell phone might ring at any time, as she was a professional legal counselor. But the ringing of the home phone at such an hour was something of a mystery.

"Maybe the Walkers' babysitter wants something," Martha said. After a two-second hesitation, Martha moved to push the reception button on the phone. She nearly gasped when she saw the face on the monitor: it was Magistrate Cromwell!

Cromwell began by indicating he'd noticed the shock on her face. "Martha, I apologize for this unexpected contact. Ordinarily, I would not disturb your family home evening in this manner. However, I am in need of your assistance on an urgent matter that just came to my attention. I'm afraid it cannot wait until Monday. So, I trust you'll forgive my intrusion? Your help would be invaluable to me."

Recovering some of her composure, yet churning inside because of her afternoon with Rachel, Martha did her best to appear intrigued and professionally concerned, but to keep her demeanor as cool and detached as Cromwell's. It was challenging for her to switch so suddenly into lawyer mode, after her emotionally draining afternoon with Rachel, and then the rich Saturday evening meal with Jacob and the Walkers. The comforting dinner of pasta with mushroom cream sauce, followed by her favorite tart-cherry pie, had made her feel lazy and relaxed. She knew she could not afford to be at less than her best with Cromwell. A surge of adrenaline took away her sleepy edge.

"Of course, Magistrate. What can I do to assist you?"

"Well, as you and Rachel DeLine share friendship, I thought it might be wise to ask if she has spoken with you recently?"

"Magistrate, we speak with one another almost every day. Why would it matter if we had spoken yesterday, or today? Have you asked Rachel?" Her mellow, musical voice was light, as she tried not to betray her first suspicion that Cromwell somehow knew about Beth.

"Martha, I just tried," Cromwell said, his expression and tone paternal, concerned. "But I could not speak with her. She has suddenly gone missing, and her husband does not know where she might be."

At those words, Martha no longer felt the need, nor the ability to hide her shock and fear. "This would be my natural reaction, even if I knew nothing," she thought desperately to herself, as her knees wobbled and she grabbed one of the dining chairs, to collapse onto its seat. The only word she could get out was: "What?"

"That's right, Martha. And to help find her, we are trying to discover what might lie behind her sudden disappearance. While we presume this is involuntary, and perhaps some criminal has, for whatever reason, taken her against her will, we cannot yet rule out some voluntary decision by her to disappear, strange though that would seem. Her husband indicates shock and dismay that Rachel never returned home today, from the center. So, when did you last speak with her? In recent conversations, did she reveal anything that might help explain this?"

Martha took a deep breath, and then another, to steady herself. "Magistrate, I last spoke with my friend Rachel on the telephone yesterday. That exchange had nothing unusual to it. And I can't think of anything, just now, that seemed to come up in any recent conversations."

"Nothing about a teenage girl she suddenly took

home as a houseguest?"

A cold shock ran down Martha's spine. "What?"

"Yes. According to the examiner who questioned John, this girl was a runaway from an orphanage, and Rachel was trying to get her off the streets. But the girl ran off, and has also disappeared. Yet, Rachel has not contacted you today? And all of this is news to you?" The question sounded genuine, not ironic or skeptical. Martha had no idea what to think. Cromwell was very good at what he did; she knew that much.

"Magistrate, I am sorry. I am in the dark on this. And I am shocked. I'm worried for my friend Rachel. Oh, how are John and Maggie? Maybe I should go to see them!"

"They are being attended to and cared for, I assure you. Martha, you will have to stay put, and await the law steward who has been dispatched to come to you to obtain your sworn testimony."

"Oh yes, of course, Magistrate."

"Don't worry, Counselor, we will find Rachel. Then, we will get to the bottom of all of this. I bid you good night, and God's peace."

As the transmission ended, Martha gave in to her avalanche of emotion, and buried her face in her hands. Rob and Susan were perfectly still, trying to accept the reality of the situation. Jacob was the one who was most stunned. Still holding one end of the board-game box he'd never completely placed down on the table, he was staring at Martha. His expression was like that of a young child who had just discovered that Santa Claus was really "just Daddy in a costume." Jacob had never before experienced any falsehood in his wife. Never. Yet, he had just watched her lie with startling boldness, to the highest authority in the entire region! Who was this woman? Just how extensive was her falsehood? What on earth was going on right under his nose?

But at that moment, the most urgent matter for his attention was getting rid of Rob and Susan. So, Jacob decided to step over by Martha; placing his hand on her shoulder, he looked at their friends with a pleading look on his face, and said, "I am sorry, friends -- but it looks like our evening has been cut short." Of course, the Walkers were completely in agreement, and with sympathetic expressions, they quickly departed. Inside the McIntosh home, a time of reckoning was needed, before the arrival of the appointed law steward. Martha knew she was doomed. She looked up into Jacob's troubled dark eyes, and knew also that she had irrevocably damaged her marriage.

⸺≫«(●)»≪⸻

CHAPTER SIX

In Colorado Springs, at the intersection of Prospect and Paseo, there stood an ordinary office building. Inside the building, on the ground floor, were the offices of Martha K. McIntosh, legal counselor. Very late on a Saturday night, those offices were ordinarily vacant. However, at this late hour, two female figures occupied the shadows within. They did not belong there, yet had been granted entrance in the form of a keypad access code.

Rachel and Beth had arrived there only an hour after the evening newscast had concluded. As they hid they talked, going over their plans for escape. Their plan was to try to get to neutral Mormon territory in Salt Lake City, and from there to Washington State, which had seceded from the theocratic United States and was now part of Canada. They would catch the first morning train to Denver, and change trains there for Salt Lake. Because the next morning would be Sunday, there was no choice for the two women but to leave in the middle of this very night. For as soon as it was Sunday morning, there would no longer be any possibility of avoiding detection hiding at the DeLine house.

The window blinds were slightly opened in each of the series of five windows that lined the long wall facing Paseo Road. Rachel and Beth sat in chairs next to the opposite wall, in dark shadows, where they could see the street outside without being seen. Speaking in hushed voices, they had reached a quieter, calmer moment in the course of their discussion, when Beth suddenly changed topics.

"Rachel, you're a reverend, right?"

"Yes, my dear. I've been a commissioned servant of the church all of my adult life."

Beth felt that at last she could safely voice the confusion that had haunted her for so long. "So you pretty much understand the church, right? Why are these church people so hard, and so scary?"

"Hmmm. Yes, I know the church, but that's not the same as understanding what the church has become. Actually, Beth, the church as it is right now has been this way only since just before the time you were born. When I was your age, there were many different and separate churches, all worshipping Christ and following his teachings – though in many different ways.

"The church I grew up in believed women could be ordained ministers and leaders of the church. The writings in the Holy Bible were important to us and our faith, but we did not consider them 'infallible,' totally perfect and unquestionable, dictated from the mind and the 'mouth' of the Lord Almighty. And infallibility is the idea that has changed everything about the church. Over a long period of time, Beth, almost a hundred years – more and more Christians came to see the Bible as a perfect authority.

"I suppose they felt they needed to trust in its perfect authority, so they would not have to rely on their own minds and hearts for interpretation of the truth and wisdom found in the scriptures. They began to view the human mind and human heart, human wisdom, as things to be mistrusted. So, the church was changing even as I was growing up. Although, really, I suppose it all began even sometime before that. Anyway, the needs of people for the safety of order, and the security of rules, moved our entire society to where we are now."

Beth listened carefully. She understood why people wanted rules and order; she wanted those things, too. But it was much harder for her to imagine why people would turn away from trusting their hearts.

"We have unchallengeable law and order, we have strict codes of decency, and we have more safety and security than ever before. But it now seems clear to me that we have gone too far. It seems to me that – in our drive to be pure and perfect, safe and secure, we have lost the mercy, the compassion of Christ. There is less wisdom now than before. And it seems that we love laws and order MORE than we love our neighbors."

Beth nodded. It was a relief to her to hear Rachel say what she had so often thought – that the church seemed to have very little to do with Jesus. "I see," said Beth. "I guess that explains how church people are so tough and scary. But, well, since Lord God is bigger and more powerful, and more perfect than the church, how come he doesn't fix these things that went wrong with the church?! I mean, look at me! I'm in trouble when I haven't done anything to hurt anyone! And look at you – you're running like a criminal when all you've done is help me!" She paused for a moment, and then her sweet high voice pierced Rachel's heart with a question so poignant that Rachel thought she could not bear the pain of hearing it. "Rachel? Why doesn't the Lord God of the church care about people like me?"

Rachel was too dumbstruck to say anything. She just opened her arms to receive Beth in an embrace. As the young woman leaned into her arms, Beth sobbed out the words: "I never would hurt anyone, you know?! How can I be a criminal? I can't understand!"

Softly, Rachel breathed words onto Beth's shoulder as they hugged – words she didn't even think about – they just came pouring out of her heart.

"Beth, I can't explain how big a mistake this must be. I feel that Christ cares about you more than his church people can care. And I believe these arms of mine are really Christ's way of trying to reach you with caring, and show you love, and help you not be so alone. I'm convinced that

God brought you to me for this reason. And, while I like you an awful lot – I think Christ loves you far more than I ever could."

The silence that followed enfolded the two women with everything except emptiness. Time was absent. The radiant quality of unconditional love made all matters of pain and joy irrelevant; all issues of hope and despair became nonexistent, and the world was much further away than the reality of heaven. For the first time in her life, Beth experienced a glimmer of what God's church on earth was meant to be – God's love shown through the compassion and love of God's people.

Eventually though, physical reality and human needs brought the older woman back to the shadowed office space, where the only sounds were their breathing and the gentle ticking of a clock. Rachel felt the need to stand, and to flex and stretch muscles that were stiffening. She also needed to visit the restroom.

"Beth," she said quietly, as she released the girl from her embrace, "just stay put. I'll be right back, after I take a quick look at the back door, and use the women's room. I won't be long." After a quick look of concern, Beth mutely nodded her acknowledgment. Rachel slipped quietly through the office door and out into the hallway.

Beth had passed many nights in unfamiliar surroundings, many less comfortable than that office, yet she had never before felt the pursuit of authorities bearing down on her. Never before had the shadows inside a building, created by light cast from outside the windows, looked so sinister. She had always been a "nobody," and so she had found it easy to hide in her anonymity. The danger of discovery had never pressed in on her with every little sound, and each tiny motion at the edges of her vision. Suddenly, Beth sat bolt upright, as she recognized with alarm that she was seeing and hearing real danger!

A couple of small light-ripples, cast through the regular pattern of window-blind shadows, came from across the street. These were accompanied by the muted sounds of car doors closing. Swiftly, Beth crawled across the carpeted floor, toward the doorway Rachel had recently passed through, which entered the central hallway.

Easing herself around the edge, remaining in a crouch, Beth scanned the hall for any sign of movement – especially looking for Rachel. The hallway was clear. Beth rose gradually to standing, just inside the hall beyond the edge of the doorway. This allowed her to slowly peek back around the door frame, and through the office windows to the street outside. She saw the large black van parked across the street, and several bouncing flashlight beams. Shifting her eyes back toward the hall, Beth risked a whispered yell: "RACHEL!!"

No response. No sound, no movement; nothing. But outside the building, feet and light beams were approaching. She could not hesitate -- not another second more.

NOW was the moment to dash for the back door, and to hope it was still available! She felt a stab of guilt, knowing that she was abandoning Rachel to a fate meant for them both, but she also knew that she herself was dangerous to Rachel, and so perhaps she would stand a better chance against the authorities without Beth.

She sprinted toward the backdoor, without another thought. Straight down the hall, and then to her right, to jump over the entire half-flight of steps, landing with only a slight thud just before the door. She hit the push-bar and sprinted again, all in one motion. Heedless of any lurkers beyond the door, she met none. Flying as fast as her sneakered feet could run, Beth hammered straight down the alleyway that lay directly behind the building.

As yet, no sounds were behind her: no shouts, no running steps pounding in her direction – though it was hard to hear over her own panting, and the pounding pulse in her temples. She just kept pumping her arms and legs, and hoping she wasn't making a great amount of noise. The alley continued for another block, then another, and then another.

All the yards, and all the buildings she passed, were without lights. She just kept moving at top speed, as though the hounds of hell were at her heels. But just one more block ahead, there was a tall street-light post, and her alley came to an end at that cross-street.

As she ran toward the light, she heard someone

weeping, and it took her a few seconds to realize that it was her own voice. Terror gripped her – although not with paralysis – instead, with a ceaseless impulse to move and to keep moving, as fast as she could. She was gradually slowing, though against her will. Even with all her surging adrenaline, her physical stamina was reaching a limit for all-out sprinting. She became aware of the ragged nature of her breathing and the strange new quiver in her legs, just as her arms became quite a bit heavier. So, she slightly slowed her pace, as she was forced to decide whether to turn right, or to turn left, entering the illumination of the street-light as the alley dead-ended. Beth went left, and slowed her pace to a jog.

———— (◐) ————

Meanwhile, back at the office building, the lawmen were entering the front door. Having surveyed the perimeter, they stationed two lookouts (one at the front-right corner, and the other at the back-left), as the other three men entered the building. They used a government-issued "master swipe-card" on the lock. They switched off their flashlights and stood still, listening, while allowing their eyes to adjust to the dim interior. Hearing no sound, the leader signaled to one that he search the office, pointed the other to the "men's room," and indicated that he would enter the "women's room."

Rachel had been inside the women's restroom all this time. So, she did not hear Beth's urgent whisper, and discovered her peril only upon carefully opening the restroom door, moments later. Rachel saw the bobbing beams of light from the men approaching the front door. She abruptly determined that continuing into the hall would mean the risk of being caught in one of the light beams almost at the door. Closing the restroom door, she fought her panic, praying that Beth was eluding capture -- because it seemed Rachel was trapped!

Desperately, she mentally reviewed the entire space of the women's room as she remembered it with the lights on. There was a custodial closet just back over there – though it was probably locked…. Her hand found the doorknob of the closet, and felt the old-fashioned keyhole in it. But, when she turned the knob, it went with her hand – unlocked! Oh, thank you, Jesus! Carefully, without breathing, she opened the door – and using her hands she examined the amount of space and location of objects inside – exhaling only when she determined she could fit inside without moving anything. But what about the door?! Quickly she felt the inside doorknob, and to her added relief discovered it was the "inside push and turn" type of door lock. She moved gingerly into the closet, closing the locked door behind her. The roots of her hair were wet with fear-driven sweat. Two seconds later, the lights in the bathroom went on.

Martha sat by herself for a few minutes. She wondered if she were making the right decision. But she knew she was; the ties of love and loyalty she shared with Rachel were deep and lasting in ways Jacob would never understand. She had evaded his questioning about the lies she told Cromwell on the phone. Jacob could not appreciate the depth of Martha's commitment to Rachel.

Martha's mind drifted back to high school. She had been a bit awkward, a bit shy; her shining intelligence isolating her from her fellow-students. She wasn't teased or bullied, but she never quite fit in. The only place she felt truly at home was in the student choir. All her life, she had loved to sing, and her parents had encouraged her, even finding a voice teacher for her. Something different came alive in Martha when she sang; her mezzo-soprano was smooth and golden as honey, hinting at the warm heart carefully concealed behind her calm, almost prim exterior.

Rachel, who was a year older than Martha, stood next to her in the alto section. The choir director immediately heard the beautiful potential of Martha's pure, lyrical voice paired with Rachel's rich, velvety contralto, and made sure that the two had opportunities to sing duets. Martha had never met anyone like Rachel, who was so spontaneously loving, so vibrantly alive, so seemingly without fear. She felt as if she were more herself when she was with the older girl, who always brought out the best in those she influenced.

Rachel persuaded Martha to volunteer with her at church summer camp, as a junior counselor. The more Rachel talked about it, the more it wonderful it sounded – ten weeks at a Christian youth camp in the Colorado mountains - surrounded by nature, giving her an opportunity to use her natural intelligence and authority where it would be accepted and appreciated. Martha agreed, and later looked back on the first two summers as the best days of her life. She and Rachel became closer than ever, and the experiences they shared were unforgettably intense… singing and praying in God's outdoor chapel of trees and towering mountains, problem-solving with kids and team-building with fellow-counselors and adult mentors, practicing care-giving skills with kids who were homesick, ill, or injured…and, of course, meeting the best kinds of boys who were also junior counselors on the camp staff.

In 2052, as Martha packed her duffel bag for her third year as a counselor, she wondered whether Jacob McIntosh would be there again this year. They had met toward the end of the previous summer, and Martha felt a rush of excitement when she thought about him. She was sixteen now, and felt much older than she had last year…old enough to see Jacob through the eyes of a young woman, rather than the eyes of a girl. She wondered if they might share one of the chaste, affectionate summer romances that so often bloomed at the camp under the watchful eyes of the older staff.

But when she saw him again, the force of his presence hit her hard, and left her breathless. At seventeen, Jacob was different from the other boys. His red hair made him stand out in a crowd, and his bold-featured face, with its prominent nose, was full of character. He seemed just as enchanted with her as she was with him, and as the sweet June days lengthened, they found more and more excuses to steal moments together, to push boundaries, to touch, to kiss, to break rules that seemed more and more foolish as the intoxication of first love overtook them.

Late one night, under a diamond-glittering canopy of stars, they sank to the ground, legs and arms, and lips entangled, with nothing in the world around them but the spicy balsam perfume of the pines, and the solid support of the earth under their yearning bodies. They were driven by hormones and desire, but more than that, they needed to be a part of each other; they were in love, and they were desperate to be as close as two people could. A voice of warning, a far-off bell, tolled in a remote corner of Martha's mind, but it belonged to another world. This was here and now – this passion, this profound knowing - this surrender.

But the next day as she sat in chapel, praying and singing, she felt shame, and fear. She didn't truly regret what she had done – it had been, in its own way, spiritual – but she was acutely conscious of having sinned. And following that consciousness was the awareness that sin had consequences. *The wages of sin is death.* Those words echoed in her mind again and again, no matter how she tried to chase them away. Pregnancy, not death, was the more likely result of her error…but what about those black vans? What if something happened and Jacob refused to support her? Terrified and alone, Martha told Rachel what had happened. Revealing her mistake to her best friend was the hardest thing she had ever done. She admired Rachel so much, and feared her friend's judgment. But once she had finished telling Rachel what had happened, the only thing she saw in her friend's clear brown eyes was light.

"I hope, for your sake, that there are no consequences," Rachel said, "but if there are, I will be here for you, now and always. I love you, Martha." She put her arms around her friend, and Martha relaxed a little in the blessing of grace, extended from a loving heart.

At the beginning of August, Martha was more in need of that grace and love than ever before. Her period was two weeks late, and she feared the worst. A pregnancy test confirmed her fears. Rachel stood by her through the whole ordeal; even going with her when Martha told her parents what had happened. She helped Martha to plan the quick wedding that was needed before the pregnancy became obvious. Jacob was surprised, but seemed genuinely willing to take on the responsibilities of husband and father. Martha noticed, though, that he seemed a little jealous of her bond with Rachel, as if it threatened him in some way. Rachel was the Maid of Honor at their wedding, and spent many happy hours with Martha learning about pregnancy and babies. Later, Martha thought that this experience they had shared was the catalyst for Rachel's calling in her ministry to mothers.

But all that learning and planning was to end in heartbreak for Martha; and for Jacob, as it turned out. A month after the wedding, she was rushed to the hospital with severe bleeding. Rachel and Jacob were both by her side during the aftermath of the miscarriage, while the doctors ran tests to make sure that Martha was healthy. Martha would never forget the frozen look on Jacob's face when the doctor told them that Martha's blood test showed a lupus-related rheumatoid factor that would always cause problems with carrying a baby to full term. The odds were heavy that she would always miscarry at around the 20-week mark. She and Jacob would never have natural children of their own.

Martha felt something in herself change after that. She was still so young, but a door had closed with brutal finality. Although she and Jacob continued to build their relationship, she always felt that somehow he blamed her for the loss of the dream of children. She couldn't bring herself to ask about it. Their childlessness remained a touchy subject. Martha couldn't bear the idea of adoption, and Jacob did not press her. Rachel remained Martha's touchstone of faith, sanity, and support through her grief and doubts. She didn't even blame Martha when, upon learning of Rachel's own pregnancy, Martha had unexpectedly stormed out of the room, angry beyond all reason, not at her friend, but at fate. Rachel understood. Rachel always understood – truly understood, from a depth of compassion in her heart that awed Martha - and scared her a little bit, too. She had wondered for a long time whether someday Rachel's open-heartedness would get her into trouble.

Well, it seemed that day had arrived; and Martha was ready to stand by Rachel, just as Rachel had always stood by her. Without further hesitation, Martha made her way to her parked car, and drove away from home, and toward shared danger with Rachel.

————)((•)) ————

Beth had jogged, then walked, nine blocks to the west. As she approached a more brightly lighted intersection, she noted that the street sign read "NEVADA." The street was empty of traffic, of course, as the clock approached midnight. Momentarily, she thought of the Nevada Transit Line on the metro-rail – but quickly discarded that idea as an almost certain way to get caught and arrested. She had to keep moving! Where, though? What was happening with Rachel? Would she ever see her again? How would they ever hook up in the days ahead – while both of them were running from the law? That could happen only if Rachel had also gotten away. Did she hear voices?! Beth stepped back further into the shadows, and studied the brightly lit area across the street – it was a hospital. That meant there would be some alert and active people around there. Worse, the area was so much more brightly lit that she'd be easily seen and reported to the authorities if anyone happened to look her way. But she couldn't turn around. And going along the major avenue of Nevada would assure that a law steward van would soon be along. Oh, how to choose? Still, she couldn't stay; she needed to pick a path and get going.

Her eyes spotted what seemed to be a bicycle lying on the grass near the Emergency Room doors. Yes – it was! And yet, the hospital was a place she'd most likely be seen by someone. Could she risk it? If she got the bike, it would be worth the risk. If not – well, then it was all over and done.

Beth stared at the bicycle with fear and wonderment, and hesitation. All children were taught to ride bicycles, even at the orphanage, as it was the main mode of transportation. She had been a good, strong rider, and was confident that if she could get the bike, she would be in a good position to put some much-needed distance between herself and the law stewards. In her young life, Beth had never before stolen anything more than a piece of food. But, well, she was already running from the law, wasn't she? So, bracing herself for the illumination, and the act of theft, she walked as "normally" as she could straight for the bike. It occurred to her to make it seem like she was just retrieving her own ride, as she moved her eyes all around (but not her head) to spot anyone looking her way. She saw no people as she reached the bicycle, and she heard no sounds at all. Upon closer examination, the bike was a good fit for her needs – it was a woman's bike, and not too new…it was an older model, originally painted dark blue, but it had some worn paint. Bending down, she got the bicycle up, and walked with it to the street she'd been following. She was now on the other side of Nevada Avenue. Still no alarm had sounded, so she mounted the bike and began pedaling west.

⸻ ((◉)) ⸻

CHAPTER SEVEN

Rachel had no idea how long she spent in that closet. But when she could tolerate it no longer, she gently turned the doorknob and eased the door open a crack. The lights had been left on, and their brilliance at first hurt her eyes. Rachel hesitated long enough to allow her eyes to adjust. Then, she very slowly opened the door the rest of the way. As quietly as she could, she moved first one foot and then the other, leaving the shelter of the closet.

Standing quite still, she listened intently for any sounds beyond the bathroom door. After a full minute, Rachel moved toward the door and turned the light switch off. She listened for another long minute with her ear near the door. Then, very gradually, she opened the door a crack to a dark hallway. She stood very still within the door frame. Her eyes were now readjusted to the dark, and she moved them with care over her entire view of the building interior. As she still had not heard nor seen anything suspicious, Rachel crouched down and eased the restroom door further open. Moving in a crouched position, she made her way to the front entry windows surrounding the front door.

Could it possibly be that Rachel had outlasted the searchers? The black van was gone from across the street. But how many men might have been left behind? There still might be two or three carefully positioned watchers, who were waiting to capture anyone seen entering or leaving the building. In any case, it was a sure thing that the authorities had the building's security cameras online and ceaselessly monitored.

Sooner or later, she'd be forced to risk either the front door or the back door. Rachel had to escape, and begin her search to discover what had happened to Beth. And yet, getting herself captured would not serve the cause, either. What to do? How could she choose? She felt paralyzed, a feeling she was not familiar with. It was rare for Rachel not to have a clear sense of what to do next; she almost always knew the best course of action. This was not arrogance or overconfidence on her part; it was simply that her heart was a beacon, always shining toward what was right, and she had learned to trust herself. But this was different. What was right, and what was possible, were two different things. Just at that moment, Rachel's vision was attracted to movement on the street. Down the way, and across the intersection, she saw a familiar vehicle parked; it had flashed its headlights on and off, as if to get her attention. It was the four-passenger sedan belonging to Martha McIntosh!

Her choice was made. It was time to go. Rachel knew the front-door security camera would show her exiting the building, but there was no avoiding that. She did pray that for the next four seconds, someone monitoring that view-screen would have their attention focused elsewhere.

Rachel shoved at the push bar, and moved as fast as she could through the door, and to her left along the sidewalk. Then, she bolted diagonally across the street intersection, sprinting for the McIntoshs' sedan. Reaching the passenger door, and without looking inside, she jerked it open and threw herself in.

Martha did not wait for the door to close, and abruptly pulled away from the curb. She had started the ignition the moment she saw Rachel emerge from the building. She followed that block of Madison Street until she could make the sharp right turn onto Templeton Gap; then, crossing La Salle, she took the first left. Her intent was for Prospect Street to absorb them into a separate neighborhood from where they had begun. She drove with her headlights off; the car was dark gray, and it passed through the streets like a quiet ghost. Only when they were rolling modestly along a quiet neighborhood street did Martha glance over at her friend.

Rachel was staring at the Emergency-Band Radio attached to the car's dashboard. From the radio she heard: "…search parties pursuing fugitives named Rachel DeLine, and Beth Laham." The look on Rachel's face was absolute bewilderment and shock. Seeing this, Martha spoke softly. "From the years before the new social order. Most criminal lawyers had them. It's just an oversight, I'm sure, that these haven't been confiscated. In those days, we attorneys were considered an integral part of the legal system."

Her speech seemed to break the spell paralyzing Rachel. She looked at Martha, blankly at first, and then rapidly she shifted to a flood of thoughts and emotions.

"Martha, oh my God! I can't believe you…how did you know to…oh, to have you get me away just then? Martha! What are you doing? Are you crazy? Now you're a criminal, too!"

"Easy, Rachel, calm down. We are lawbreakers, and we have been for almost two days." Martha's voice was calm and steady; she knew she had to be grounded for both of them. She could almost see the surge and swirl of Rachel's tumultuous emotions. "But I don't know where Beth is! We have to…"

"Rachel, I do have an idea where she's headed. They don't have her yet…but, she's been spotted…"

"Dear Lord!"

"…west of here. She's pedaling a bicycle toward the hills of God's Garden. The radio. Remember?"

"Oh, yeah. Riding a bike? But…"

Martha interrupted kindly but firmly. "Rachel, please! The radio—we need to listen."

Rachel just nodded her head in reply. Then she focused on looking ahead, and along her side of the street, for any sign of Beth on a bicycle.

———————⋙«(●)»⋘———————

Beth was pedaling the bicycle as fast as she could. She was sure she had been seen by that law steward a few blocks before, as she had crossed the intersection at Centennial Boulevard. It was difficult to gain great speed, however, as the bike seat and handlebars were not adjusted to her size.

The winding neighborhood street was still bearing west, and so she leaned into the effort as the street names came and went. Vondehl Park Drive became Michener Drive, which then became Kissing Camels drive. And that street was now bending mostly southward, so when it intersected with Hill Circle she banked a hard right toward the mountains, once again.

Her breath was coming in ragged panting now, and the tight, aching knot at the bottom of her rib cage was worsening. She could tell she was nearing the end of her stamina, and that scared her. Only by reaching the rugged terrain of the red-rock foothills would she have any hope of eluding capture. For Beth, her fear of being gobbled up by a black van was converted into energy.

The pavement inclined more steeply upward now,

and she was aware only of her heavy legs, and her heavy breathing. Beth could not know that she was entering a region west of Colorado Springs that once was named "Garden of the Gods." Nor could she possibly know that just before reaching the immense "garden" of red-rock formations, the road she was traveling would suddenly and steeply head downward into a ravine.

As Beth labored the bike pedals to keep turning, her total awareness had tightened into focus on only the pavement in front of her. So, it took her fully three seconds to notice the remotely piloted aerial drones up in the night sky, bearing down on her position. Then, she heard the low whine, and buzzing drone of the winged robotic pursuers. And she knew that these unmanned aerobots could see her already, because they were equipped with infra red optics!

Law stewards would be on her in only a few more minutes, now. But there was no more force left in her quivering legs for speed. There was nowhere to turn, and no prospective hiding places—she was trapped in the open! And then, just as an intense light fastened on to her—blinding her with brightness—the front wheel of the bicycle abruptly lowered, following the downward incline of the road. Beth instantly found her full weight tilted toward the handlebars, with the back wheel lifting momentarily from the pavement. For a second, the bright illumination of the spotlight fell away from her, and she plunged into complete darkness.

Her momentum was too great —and she went wide outside the road shoulder. Fighting for control of the speeding bike, as it slid on gravel and dirt, she screamed when the front wheel slid over the edge.

————)(◐)(————

In Martha's car, she and Rachel heard the radio trans-missions indicating that the authorities were closing in on Beth. They listened intently, as Martha wheeled the ve-hicle west down Fillmore, and then north on Centennial. Then they spotted a roadblock hundreds of yards ahead. When the helicopter crew reported over the radio that they had found Beth, Rachel suddenly grabbed Martha's arm, and said, "Pull over, Martha."

Even in the dark, Rachel could see Martha's shocked expression. "What?!"

Rachel felt resolve in her soul. "Just do it, okay? Pull over, now. This is as far as you can go. I'm getting out."

"Rachel?!"

"I mean it. They've got her, or will soon! I can't abandon her. But I've got to go on foot from here. And you must keep driving your car – right on outta here. Go, Martha – get out of here!" And with that, Rachel closed the car door, turned her back to Martha, and trotted west into the shadows beyond the glow of the street light. Martha still had her mouth open for a reply, but none ever came. Only one large tear pouring out of each eye and flowing down each cheek showed her dismay. Her friend was doomed.

CHAPTER EIGHT

Beth was now off-road and barely remaining upright on the bicycle. She instinctively steered the bike even more directly straight down the slope, while standing up on the pedals, hanging on for her life! The slope was grass, dirt, and weeds, with some rock outcroppings. She knew that if she hit one of the rocks head-on, going so very fast, it would probably kill her. But there was no other option on the steep slope, at such velocity. And being killed on the bike was not the worst thing that could happen to her now.

Slowly she squeezed tighter and tighter on the rear brake, as she bumped and bounced along. And ever so gradually, she fought with the handlebars to turn them bit by bit to the left. After seconds that seemed like years, she did manage to slightly reduce speed and to slow her descent down the slope. Then, her front wheel slammed straight into a two-foot-tall rock, and she was sent flying over the handlebars several feet through the air, landing face-first in a large sagebrush. She had a momentary awareness of the pleasant smell of the plant before she lost consciousness.

Meanwhile, Beth's sudden "evasive maneuver," just as the spotlight lost her for a mere second, had vexed her pursuers. It seemed to remote operators piloting the aerial drones as though she had just abruptly vanished without a trace. So they hovered, and the spotlight was turned off while they sought her with infra red sensors.

Moments later, Beth awoke to a poking and scratching pain several hundred yards from the searching aerobots. She hurt in more places than she had ever imagined possible. It hurt even to breathe. And it seemed too much effort to pick a direction for rolling herself out of the sagebrush. But she did – and that activity hurt greatly, too. Lying on her back with her head below her feet, on that hard, uneven ground, Beth was sorely tempted to quit, and just lie there until she was found. But, in her mind's eye she saw the caring faces of Rachel, and Maggie, and John. In them, she had seen that life could be more than what she had experienced. She wanted such things as love, trust, and hope. Rachel had risked so much for her – she owed it to her to try until she truly could try no more.

So she rolled over to painfully push up to her knees. And then, spinning half-around, so her feet were down the slope, she rolled back onto her haunches. She slowly stood, swaying only slightly, while trying to get her eyes to focus, as she felt her left hip and knee complain loudly.

Beth saw the sagebrush that had saved her from worse damage, and then she cast about for some sight of the bicycle. Finally she spotted it, lying crumpled, twisted and useless. It was lying only a body-length from her left shoulder. She had to leave it. Still, maybe she could hide it first.

With all the strain it cost her, Beth bent down to grab the bent frame of the bike, and began dragging it toward a juniper bush that looked big enough to use as cover. It took half a minute to get the bike shoved under the lower side of that bush, and she was keenly aware of each second. Her hands felt clumsy; between the cold night air and her fall, she felt as if her body were moving with unnatural slowness. Then, she turned directly away from the sounds of the buzzing drones just over the ridge, and limped as swiftly as she could, diagonally downward along the slope. A sharp, hot pain pulsed from her hip down her leg with every step, but she gritted her teeth and ignored it.

She was nearing the bottom of the hill, just as the aero-bots began to fly toward her. Beth came upon a dry creek bed, with slightly bigger bushes more frequently spaced along it. Lumbering awkwardly down into the creek bed, she continued limping along its course, until suddenly it was there, right in front of her: a small stone bridge. Obviously it was very old, yet it was not crumbling down. Although it had been large enough for only one horse and cart to cross, centuries ago when it had been built, it was just big enough for Beth's purpose. With weeds so thick and tall around it, she had some difficulty getting situated under it. The rough stone bruised and scraped her hands and face, already bruised and bleeding from her fall. She carefully readjusted the weeds behind her, and drew herself underneath, just as the drones approached her hiding place under the bridge.

Rachel had, on many occasions, jogged and biked along the trails through the westernmost neighborhoods of Colorado Springs, so she was able to bypass the streets and intersections blocked by the law stewards. The pedestrian trails were well-paved, while cutting directly between houses, going underneath larger streets, and it gave Rachel a direct route to "God's Garden." She avoided detection and made good time in approaching the area where Beth had been reported.

As Rachel panted her way up a slope and around a bend in the trail, she was behind the commotion of a search, and the droning buzz of aerobots she'd been hearing for some time. The manner in which both were moving gave her the impression they were not locked on to Beth, but rather searching for her once again. Could it be that they still had not captured Beth?! She could barely dare to hope so.

Scanning the dark region north of her, and to the west, she did not observe anyone nearby. The trail continued west, tunneling beneath 30th Street, and into the enormous "hogback" of rough red-rock terrain. Though she could not see the other end of the tunnel, Rachel decided to risk it, as she needed to get west of the helicopter search. Once within those red rock formations, she would probably have a far better chance of eluding the searchers. And, she hoped, she would have some possibility of reconnecting with Beth.

The aerobots, (there seemed to be two) with their predatory probing, seemed to hover almost directly over Beth's hiding place – forever! Just when she felt she could endure no more, the drones seemed to move past and farther out, toward the hills. She became conscious of how little she was breathing, and risked a full exhale. Drawing a deep breath, she began to flex and release the muscles of her toes, then her ankles and feet, and then her knees and thighs. After a full minute of this, she dared to move for a look back where she'd been, before the bridge. Very slowly, she rolled onto her stomach, and carefully, gradually moved the tall weed stems, one by one, until she could see the dry creek bed.

She did not see any figures, nor detect any movement, for one long minute. So she undid her move, just as slowly and carefully, to do the same for a look from under the opposite side of the bridge, viewing the ground she next needed to cover. Again, she did not perceive any searchers within her sight. So it seemed to her that it was time to risk the open, once again.

Beth began a gradual "belly crawl," like soldiers were trained to do. She eased along the arm and leg of first one side, and then the opposite side. Very slowly, only inches with each movement, she made her way out from under the bridge, until she was clear. Then, she paused to listen for any sounds on the hillside, nearby. She heard nothing more than the whisper of the night wind in the weeds and grasses. She raised to her hands and knees, crawling that way a little farther, then pausing again.

Still hearing no nearby sounds, she raised herself to a crouching stance, and took a look around. She could hear people farther up and back along the slope, but she heard and saw no one nearby. The aerobots were now more than a football field away, and to the north of her, on the other side of the ridge. Looking directly toward the hills, she saw that she was near a road she would have to cross, to reach the rock garden. As she was looking, the headlights and the sounds of cars emerged from the south. The cars seemed almost a mile away, but they were approaching fast. It was time to run!

Beth bolted as vigorously toward the road as her tired legs allowed. She tried not to worry about catching her foot and stumbling, only pounding hard to reach and to cross the pavement. In a matter of seconds, she reached the raised shoulder of the road, and she labored up the embankment, and onto the asphalt; she glanced south to see the headlights now only about two hundred yards away. With a fresh rush of adrenaline, she sprang for the other side of the road, reaching it in just a few strides.

There, she stumbled and rolled down the embankment of the western side. Yet, without hesitating, she rose back to a standing crouch, and began running along the trough-like ditch next to the road. After only a few yards, and just as the tires and motors seemed to arrive, she discovered a large drainage culvert on her left, and without a blink of thought, threw her entire body inside.

She could see the lighter gray of an opening at the other end, so she began moving, in a crouch, for that opening. Behind her, she heard a couple of car-door slams, and voices. Yet, she tried to ignore that, and just kept moving as quietly as possible for the other end of a large corrugated tube. She gagged silently; the culvert was full of the stench of rotting leaves and a couple of dead rats, their yellow teeth bared in a grimace of decay.

Beth reached the opening on the far end, and climbed gingerly out. She discovered the ground was covered with noisy pea-sized gravel. Two other realizations instantly impacted Beth: first, she was on the opposite side of a rock ridge from the road; and second, she was very near the larger rock formations of God's Garden. She could hardly believe that she was making it to her goal – and she would soon have a real chance of eluding her pursuers!

———))((———

Rachel saw three government vehicles racing north on 30th Street, from her high vantage point amid the rocks. She stopped and observed them long enough to see where the first one parked, and then the second only a hundred yards farther on. Somewhere between the two cars, was the general area where the lawmen were sure Beth would be found. So, Rachel decided, she would head straight north, to the west of the road, and maybe find Beth before they did. She repeated silent prayers over and over in her mind as she walked. "Let me find her first. Let her be safe. Thy will be done, Lord."

———))((———

CHAPTER NINE

As Beth climbed the small trail that wound its way up through the rocks, which was actually a dry creek bed that became a small stream during every spring run-off, her legs were heavy with fatigue and her tongue was dry from exertion. She was forced to concentrate extremely hard on her breathing, to avoid making the louder noises of panting, gasping, and grunting. From time to time, she paused – both to catch her breath, and to listen for any pursuit. She heard sounds of searchers, though distant and faint. It seemed she was getting some separation.

Slower and slower she climbed, as she ascended a ridge of rock taller and steeper than any she'd yet encountered. After pausing once more, to gather herself for the final fifteen feet or so to cross beyond yet another rock barrier between her and her pursuers, Beth willed her fading strength to the task of gripping the rock face with her hands, while edging her feet slowly along a rock outcropping. One arm's length, and one toehold at a time, she moved around a topmost rim of the rock mountain. And then, she was around to the western side, where there was a larger rock ledge to stand upon. Her aching, quivering muscles refused to relax.

Suddenly, just below her cliff-side perch, appearing as though right at her feet, a dozen tiny house-lights came on, all at once! It must have been an exceptionally large house, as it stood at the mouth of the canyon – at least a mile below, and about that far south of Beth's position. As more of its inside and outside lights snapped on, it began to look like a castle to her eyes. The combination of startled bewilderment and exhaustion betrayed her at that moment, along with the human instinct to lean toward anything at which one stares. Beth lost her balance. She fell so abruptly, so very far, and so uninterrupted – that her tired, dry throat permitted no scream.

⸺⬦⸺

As Rachel edged through a narrow crevice between red rock boulders, she found herself overlooking a much wider canyon than the draw she'd been traversing. This canyon was filled with lights at the bottom, far below her position. She paused, and knelt down on one knee. Looking and listening, Rachel made out the shadowy figures of a dozen people – all of them moving in every direction. They seemed to be pouring forth from the big building that was the source of the many floodlights producing most of the illumination.

She held still, catching her breath, and observing the scene below her. "They are searching," she thought. "That means they still don't have her." With a deep breath, full of relief, she found the resolve to continue her own search. She moved carefully down the slope, angling away from the lights and the searchers. Rachel headed for the canyon floor, thanking divine providence for her lifelong physical fitness discipline. She hustled along to stay farther up the canyon than the swarm of searchers with their electric torches.

While she crossed the small gulley that formed the bottom, or floor, of the upper canyon, she was suddenly surprised by the sound of a low human groan. It came from directly ahead of her. As soundlessly as she could, Rachel moved in the direction of the moaning. If she had heard someone, it was not one of the searchers, so…it just might be…

That thought never finished forming, because Rachel was abruptly tripped, and fell over some knee-high object she had not seen in the dark. With a gasp, she went headfirst over a bale of spongy, crunchy, scratchy *hay!* And though a hay bale was fairly typical for such a ranching area, it nevertheless surprised Rachel.

Even though her left shoulder absorbed most of the fall, Rachel was more worried about the amount of noise she might have made with her misstep. She held herself very still, and listened intently for searchers responding to her stumble. But after more than a minute, Rachel determined that none were yet approaching. Instead, what she heard again was the sound of someone's low groan – like a sleeper dreaming of something disturbing. It came from above Rachel, and farther back along the canyon wall. She discovered that the direction of the sound seemed to be located atop a giant stack of baled hay, which Rachel soon was climbing.

Upon reaching the topmost layer of hay bales, Rachel paused in a crouch, to look and listen for pursuit. Still, there seemed no indication that any searchers had discovered her activity or location. Another barely audible groan issued from directly in front of Rachel – and this time it was clearly the sound of pain. There she was! It had to be Beth whose slight form lay sprawled upon the hay bales. The girl looked badly injured. She must have fallen!

Rapidly, on hands and knees, Rachel crawled across the several bale tops between them and reaching the side of the girl, Rachel had to bite her finger to keep from crying out her dismay. Beth's little body was so obviously broken! The arm and lower leg on her right side both jutted out at unnatural angles. The scent of blood filled Rachel's nostrils, as she maneuvered herself to lean in close over the girl's face. Beth emitted another visceral moan of pain, low and deep from within. Rachel was struck hard by the thought, "She's dying!" Rachel sat back down, and it was then that she put her hand into a copious pool of sticky, congealing blood next to Beth's broken body.

"Oh, my God!" Without another thought, Rachel was up on her feet, and shouting at the limit of her lungs: "Help! Help! Over here!"

———«(●)»———

CHAPTER TEN

John was opening the door of the Martha McIntosh's car when Maggie stirred in her child safety seat in the back. "Daddy, where are we?"

He turned to her, and spoke in a whisper. "We are at your Granny Odie's."

"Why, Daddy? It's so dark."

"Darlin', Daddy just needs you to keep quiet, as we go wake Granny up, and see her inside. Okay?"

As the familiar form of a gray tabby cat jumped on her, Maggie was not quiet. "Esmeralda?! You're here?!"

"Maggie, please – shhh, honey!" John whispered intensely. "Your kitty had to come, because we're going on a long trip, and may be gone a long time. You have more questions – but, no – those will have to wait." And, with that John picked up Maggie, who held on to the cat, and the three went to a side window of the small house.

Lightly, John tapped on the glass several times. Soon, the small glow of a bedside lamp came on. Then, one edge of the drape was slightly pulled back, until Odie's face came into view. Without a word, the elderly woman took an extensive look at the trio near her window, and then she let go of the drape. Pretty soon, they were all around a kitchen table, with only a stove light for illumination, as John began to talk. It was hard to break this news to her; she had been as kind and warm to John as if he were her own son, and he hated to tell her that her daughter was in danger.

"Odie, there's only a small chance that Rachel will get Beth out of the region. But, if they make it, Rachel is going to meet us in Spokane, Washington. Martha McIntosh, bless her soul, gave us her car. She knows she is going to be arrested for helping Rachel, so she made this final sacrifice for us. Luckily I learned to drive before the new government took over. From Spokane, with the help of your relatives, we will try for Vancouver, British Columbia. If we remain here, we will be collected by black vans, and deported to Judas Island, for sure. Rachel and Beth's only chance is to head for the trains, right away – and get on the first one headed for Salt Lake!"

⸺⸺•《●》•⸺⸺

Magistrate Jerry Cromwell was seated at his desk, lost in aimless thought. As his eyes traced the lines of wood grain on the desktop, his mind floated from one fear to another.

"This happened on my watch! Such chaos! Damn

Rachel DeLine! Why does the woman present such a challenge? How public has this disobedience become? Can I keep it quietly corralled? Well, every challenge is from Father God Almighty, and had some divine purpose. Perhaps my proper handling of this situation will more than restore the heavenly order of this parish. Perhaps this will also enhance my position within the quorum."

He looked at, not through, the large window across the office from his desk. As the midnight sky was dark outside, only his reflection in the well-lit office was framed therein. Staring back at him was a man facing difficult responsibility, and a challenging situation. He closed his eyes, and he began to assume the still, quiet posture of prayer.

As he presented his thoughts and feelings to the divine spirit, seeking peaceful clarity of wisdom that flowed from only the Lord God, Cromwell felt the struggle with doubts just fall away. Gradually, he accepted the evidence of absolute law, and the result was a solid crystallization, supporting his heart and mind. The mind of Father God's judgment would be applied to both disobedient women: that must happen. Whether that administration of holy law was public, or private, the collective wisdom of the quorum would determine. Cromwell would perform his duties as he always did, and Christ the Lord was trustworthy for the results.

Cromwell's meditation was suddenly disrupted by the

beeping tones of his official phone. Switching open the link, he was pleased to hear the voice of his chief law steward, who was leading the search for the fugitives.

"Magistrate, we have them both."

Cromwell nodded, satisfied. "Well done, my good man. You are, I trust, transporting them separately to detention?"

"Magistrate, the young woman is badly injured and we are sending her directly to the ER at Penrose. I am personally taking the older offender to the public lockup, downtown." Cromwell planned to visit Penrose as soon as it was feasible to do so. The ER there knew to keep a sharp eye out for illegal pregnancies, as it was not uncommon for frightened women with pregnancy complications to end up at the hospital.

"Chief, I'd prefer that you deliver Mrs. DeLine directly here to me -- in cuffs and shackles, of course."

"Of course, Magistrate. The Lord's will be done."

"Of course. I will meet you when you arrive. Goodbye."

And with that, the quite mortal-looking man reflected in the window of Cromwell's office switched off the phone on the desk.

At Penrose hospital, an ambulance turned into the emergency entrance, and quickly reached a stop in front of the glass double doors standing open. Two nurses were in position at the doors for the patient transfer, and their faces barely registered any surprise as the ambulance driver read to them the report of extensive damages to the anatomy of the young woman, whose broken body was being unloaded by the emergency medics who had created the report. They were busy keeping Beth alive, as they unloaded and wheeled the gurney toward the doors. The hospital ER nurses followed in quick pursuit, even though the outlook was grim: the patient could not be expected to survive much longer.

In the back seat of the black van in which she rode, Rachel was too worried for Beth even to feel her own terror. The girl had no one to care about her! This could not be okay with the heavenly Father of Christ Jesus! Beth was a tragically disconnected human soul, and should not be blown about by circumstances -- like some tumbleweed blowing in the wind. Clearly, the social order could not love Beth; it cared only about her compliance with the code of law. And circumstances had brought Beth to Rachel, and to Rachel's little family. Didn't that have the fingerprints of the Holy Spirit all over it? Oh God, Beth's injuries had been so shockingly severe! The amount of blood the girl had lost! "Merciful Lord! – please see to her care, and preserve her."

Suddenly, the van turned to the left and hit a speed bump without slowing down. Rachel was jostled, and aroused from her meditation. She was about to be delivered to her own doom, and that brought her fear immediately home to her. The van was moving down a long ramp to an underground entrance. The dim lighting was amber in the garage-like structure they entered. Slowing down greatly, the van moved toward a type of docking platform, with some form of a cage around a large metal door. Rachel guessed correctly that it was the portal of her destiny.

———◆(◆)◆———

Magistrate Cromwell was inside the door, and studied Rachel's appearance with a look of detached curiosity. To his eyes, the mature woman looked more like a nervous and exhausted teenager, who had been out all night long, and who now faced the consequences of her delinquency. The only differences were the restraints on her hands and feet, and the law enforcement officers guiding her along the hallway. She did not raise her eyes to meet his.

"Take her to holding cell 'B,'" he said. And with that, Rachel was shuffled past him to the end of the hall, and then steered to the left, through an open metal gate that clanged shut after her. Only then did a sound escape her:

one lonely sob. He registered the sound with satisfaction. He felt no animosity toward her personally, but she had to be taught that the law of the land must be followed – that the law of God must be followed. He had had enough of this headstrong and arrogant woman taking matters into her own all-too-capable hands.

————)((O)) ————

At the McIntosh home, as Martha returned from giving her car to Jonathan DeLine, she found Jacob engaged in hurriedly packing suitcases. "You're back," he exclaimed. "I did not expect to see you here again." He did not slow his packing activity as he continued: "You are going to be arrested – and I am not going to stick around to see that, Martha. I don't understand what could cause you to throw our lives away for Rachel's madness. But, you have, and it's done, and I don't intend to stick around for interrogation when you have betrayed me and everything we ever built together; everything we ever meant to each other. No – I'm gone."

"I gave the car to the DeLines," she said. "If you leave, you will have to find some other way to get away from me. You are betraying me, Jacob."

Jacob did not even react.Martha sat down, and said nothing more, because there was nothing to be said. She watched her husband of nineteen years walk to the door with his suitcases, and leave – without another word. She had no idea where he would go, and at that moment, she didn't care. The fact of his leaving told her that their marriage had not been what a marriage should be. They did not share values; they were not truly a partnership. Then she hung her head, and cried. Her only consolation was that they did not have children to be endangered or hurt by his behavior…or by hers.

Martha was still sitting there when law stewards arrived to arrest her.

CHAPTER ELEVEN

The dignified-looking gentleman in a trench coat, with a fedora on his head, seemed out of place at the emergency desk of Penrose Hospital. But Cromwell had come over to discover first-hand the condition of and prognosis for the young woman fugitive. He needed to discover the facts of the situation. He would be addressing the entire parish in just a few hours, during Sunday morning worship, and he would need to be prepared with full knowledge of the facts. He would craft his message with just the right slant on the incident. The message would need to demonstrate that through the magistrate, God was clearly in charge of all things.

"Yes, Magistrate, right this way, sir. I will give you a full briefing. Just follow me," said the nurse, who lifted a datapad from the other side of the counter. She gestured him toward the hallway on his left, and began moving that way. Cromwell fell into step beside her, and they made their way down the hall to a closed door on their right. When the nurse opened the door, he could see a small conference room inside. It was dominated by an oval-shaped table, with only enough room for seating around it. As he entered, she shut the door behind them. The nurse gestured him toward one of the seats as she sat in another. She placed the clipboard on the table in front of her, and in her crisp, efficient manner, she began reading from the report.

"The young woman's injuries were extensive, sir. She'd lost several units of blood and could not be roused to consciousness; her vital functions were weak and inconsistent, and ER physicians scrambled to try to stabilize her."

Cromwell interrupted: "Did she die?"

"No sir," the nurse replied, daring to look him in the face. "Not yet, at any rate. She has received the needed units of blood, along with other intravenous solutions. The uterine bleeding and vaginal hemorrhaging have been stemmed..."

Again Cromwell interrupted: "The baby was lost, then?"

"Yes sir, a traumatic miscarriage of the approximately thirteen-week pregnancy." The nurse paused, as the magistrate seemed to stare right through her. "Should I continue, Magistrate?"

"Mmm? Oh, yes, please go on."

"Well, sir, the large amount of blood loss was due primarily to the miscarriage. However, there was also some internal bleeding due to the broken ribs -- and breaks in the right leg, the right arm, and right shoulder. Her right lung was punctured, and her spleen and liver were damaged as well. It really is pretty amazing that her neck wasn't badly damaged, as well as her head. But those both escaped severe injury, even though her fall was extremely far."

"You said, she is not dead 'yet.' You seem to imply her chances of survival are slim."

"Umh, well sir, the attending surgeon would have to declare the official prognosis, and that is not in the report I have, sir."

"It seems that for the moment, I will have to settle for your 'impression.' What is your unofficial impression of her condition and likely outcome, Nurse?"

"It would take a miracle for her to survive, sir"

"Thank you, Nurse," said Cromwell, rising to his feet. "That will be all for now." He paused then, as he held the door open. Cromwell softly said, "One last thing, Nurse. I am sure the chief steward has required a DNA check on the poor deceased baby? This involves a legal matter, one that will require the search for the fornicating man who impregnated the girl. *That man* will face some severe criminal penalties."

⸺ ((◉)) ⸺

Rachel found it difficult to pray in holding cell "B." This was because of the sterile surroundings, and due to the abject terror that seized her. It was as though her mind were frozen. Only feelings of unbelievable fear claimed her soul. Rachel felt like some helpless animal whose predator had her cornered, and was slowly advancing with drooling fangs for the kill. The cell, which was like a cage in a scientist's lab, only enhanced that feeling. Every surface, every fixture, was stainless steel. Even the bunk bed on the wall was steel, with a thin mattress rolled up at one end, which she would unroll if she ever felt like trying to sleep.

Somewhere in a thin sliver of Rachel's awareness, she did register a noise beyond her cell, at some point in her hours of devastation. It sounded something like the sounds of manacled shuffling and the crying sobs of a woman. Those sounds were followed by the distinct metallic clang of another cell door being slammed. This was the only disruption of Rachel's timeless existence in cell "B."

⸻ ◈ ⸻

Worship at the Christian Temple in Colorado Springs that Sunday morning was the usual splendid pageantry of all Sundays – that is, until the final third of the worship time. This was the portion that was always the magistrate's address. When Cromwell ascended to the high pulpit and began to speak, many folks in attendance and many more watching elsewhere on viewing screens were quickly aware of the difference in the magistrate's demeanor. His calm elegance was punctuated by an air of triumph that was apparent even over his usual air of authority.

"Sisters and brothers, I greet you in the name of Jesus Christ. How glad we are for our Savior, bringing us ever closer to the New Jerusalem -- heaven on earth, as it is in God's eternal realm. Our praises are ceaseless for the Lord's goodness in guiding us to fulfill our manifest destiny as a Christian nation. Amen? That's righteous! Yes, amen.

"Now we are becoming more and more unified. Our cities, our streets, our homes, our very lives are all becoming more peaceful. The goodness of Biblical law is permeating our neighborhoods, and our markets, and our stewardship of government.

"Not that all this blessing has been without labor pains. Even still our brave and loyal soldiers of the Joshua Forces combat hostile, well-armed insurgencies at some of our borders, while nearer to home, the sense of mutiny and devilish disobedience still possesses the hearts of a few.

"I cannot tell you strongly enough just how much it breaks the heart of Jesus when anyone among us demonstrates the same mistrust and willful rebellion shown by that first sinner: Lucifer himself. This is so much worse than mere error. This is not a simple straying from the path; such sinfulness involves belligerent choosing: an abuse of free will contending against the holy will of God. To knowingly and willfully strive against the commands of Father God Almighty is the very perversion of the Archangel Lucifer, who was thrown down from heaven to the depths of hell, where he became Satan by name, and committed himself to forever contending against the goodness of the Heavenly Father's law."

As Cromwell reached that climax of his message, he paused for dramatic effect. This effect worked, and his listeners were poised for the next point.

"My dear, dear, sisters and brothers. There has been – just now -- such a transgression in our midst. Last night, mutineers against God's authority tried to defy the Almighty, willfully and with full knowledge of their crimes. They even fled from our stewards of holy law for a little while. But those fugitives were found! And while one sits unharmed in her prison cell, the other is dying, even as I speak -- though not from any actions by our law stewards -- only as a result of her own extreme efforts to escape righteous justice. Those two criminals fled and so were caught, but there is a third criminal involved, and I assure you our stewards of divine law are pursuing him. Even now, this unworthy rebel against God is not fleeing. He is trying to escape justice by hiding. However, we have his DNA and we will soon be arresting him, also."

The stillness was that of an audience completely

stunned and subdued. Cromwell did not force them to endure that for more than two seconds. Smoothly, he continued: "With our assurance of faith that God will prevail, let us continue by rising to sing, as one, song number 2091."

CHAPTER TWELVE

Rachel awoke to the sound of the prison guard unlocking her cell. She was confused, having fallen asleep the night before with her mind and heart full of prayer – not for herself, but for Beth, for Martha, for her family. She did not even pray for their safety or deliverance; her repeated prayer was one of thanks for the blessing of their presence in her life, of contrition for any suffering she had caused them, and then, finally: *Thy will be done, Lord. Thy will be done.* She could not believe that the persecution her loved ones currently faced was the work or the will of the Lord. If the Lord's will were to be done... they would be safe.

The guard had a taser at the ready in case Rachel should try to bolt. Rachel did not move from her position curled up on the bed. She knew her trial would be soon, and she did not want to compromise her physical or mental readiness for it by bringing unnecessary stress and punishment upon herself. The guard, a heavy-set woman with an expressionless face, put a bowl of water and a small brown cloth inside the door of the cell, and then locked the cell again. Rachel, who had been expecting her usual prison breakfast of glue-like oatmeal, was confused. Now that the door was locked again, she felt she could safely move without the guard being threatened.

"What--" she began, but her voice cracked from disuse.

The guard turned back toward her. "Clean yourself up," she said. "The magistrate is coming to see you."

Rachel stared blankly in the direction of the guard's retreating figure. Cromwell. He must be coming to tell her about the trial. When would he be here? A small spark of panic fluttered in her chest; although she was in jail, she valued her dignity, and she did not want to be unprepared when he arrived. She dipped a finger into the bowl of water; it was hot, unlike the ice-cold, metallic-tasting water that came from the single tap in her cell sink. She soaked the coarse washrag in the hot water, and scrubbed it vigorously across her face, and then her hands. She wet it again and tried to tame her tangled hair. Suddenly inspired, she raked her fingernails through her damp hair, and managed to tidy it into a braid. She tied the loose ends of the braid by pulling a few strands and using them like a string, which she wrapped and tied. She felt much better after this, and the sting of the rough cloth had forced her fully awake. Let Cromwell come: she was ready for him. She sat on the edge of her bed and resumed her meditation to God.

Some time later, her reverie was interrupted by the sound of footsteps clanging in the hall – two sets, this time. She saw the prison guard approaching, and the tall, imposing figure of Magistrate Cromwell. Vulnerable as she now was, she saw, more clearly than she ever had before, the force of his physical presence in his beautifully tailored suit. There was no extra weight on him, but he was square and solid, and if he had not been so dedicated to what was right, she might have worried that he would punish her himself, in some way. He was big enough, and strong enough, to do it. But she knew him well enough to know that his physical power was useful to him only insofar as it gave additional confidence to his spiritual authority.

The guard unlocked the cell. Rachel saw that Cromwell was carrying a folding chair under his arm. The guard mutely surrendered the cell key to Cromwell. "You may go," he said, and the guard's footsteps echoed away down the hall. Cromwell did not lock the cell door. Nodding to Rachel, he said, "I think you would not be so foolish as to attempt to flee while I am here." She neither agreed nor disagreed. He unfolded the chair, and sat down in it, his immense dignity in no way compromised by the awkward seating. He looked as though he had been designed as part of the furnishings of the cell; his pale-gray tailored suit and silver hair blended with the bright stainless steel all around him.

"Rachel," he said, his elegant voice holding a note of regret, as if he were truly sad to see her here. "Rachel, do you know what day it is?"

She was disoriented; she actually wasn't sure. But she did not want him to know this, so she remained silent.

"It is Tuesday morning," he continued. "Your trial is tomorrow. There are no words to tell you how deeply disappointed I am to see you here, to know that you have brought this shame upon yourself, and upon your friends and family."

"And yet, I think you will try to find words, won't you, Magistrate?" Rachel said. A spark gleamed in Cromwell's eye.

"It is my duty to speak frankly to you," he said, "but it is not within the scope of my duty to feel for you. And yet, Rachel, whether you choose to believe me or not…I do feel for you. I am aware that you see me as an inflexible mouthpiece of the government, but I am more than that. I am a man with a wife and a son, whom I love. I care for the innocent; I care about those who suffer. That is why I carry out my duty to the very letter of the law – because I know that the law is in place to protect those who cannot protect themselves." He looked sternly over the rim of his glasses at Rachel.

"But I am not unfeeling," he reiterated. "In researching who would be the best choice to replace you at the Center, I also researched you, and your work there." He shook his head. "You were correct in saying that you will be difficult or even impossible to replace. The depth and breadth of your compassion, the tireless energy with which you have worked to better the lives of those who are lost and helpless, the generosity with which you have educated mothers in order to better the lives of our next generation… well, I have nothing but admiration for the good things you have done. I know what it is like to be deeply inspired, even driven, by the will to do good. I would be proud to have a daughter like you, Rachel."

Rachel could not help responding to these kind words; they were obviously sincere. There was, in fact, more to Magistrate Cromwell than she had been willing to consider. She did not say anything in response, and she did not smile, but she felt the balm of his words dropped into the wound that was her arrest and imprisonment. It was perhaps even more painful, then, when he chose to cut her even more deeply.

"My disappointment can only be equal to my admiration," he said, an edge to his smooth voice. "You are accused on five counts. You are guilty on five counts. You are a criminal of such proportions as we rarely see in this God-fearing society. You are a danger to yourself and to those around you. Clearly, even your husband knows this. Rather than stand by you, and be condemned and doomed by your wrongdoing, he took your child and fled, hoping to save himself and her from you…he was escaping from you, Rachel."

No, she thought, *he was escaping from **you,** and everything you stand for.* "What is going to happen to me?" she asked, ignoring the lie he spoke about John.

"It will not take the tribunal long to convict you. Do you know the charges?" Rachel shook her head. Cromwell folded a finger down into his palm with each charge. "Failure to report, harboring a fugitive, resisting arrest, reckless endangerment…and accomplice to manslaughter." This last was counted on his thumb, and now his clenched fist rested in his lap. Rachel, looking at it, involuntarily moved backward. He suddenly realized what he had done, and relaxed his hand. His wedding ring gleamed as he did so. Did he really love his wife and son? Perhaps he did. But Rachel was sure that he defined love differently than she herself did.

"Manslaughter," she repeated slowly. "Beth…she's dead?"

"Bethany Laham is in a fight for her life. The doctors, nurses, and surgeons who attend her around the clock see some hope of her survival. But no…can you not guess who died?"

Rachel closed her eyes, remembering the pool of blood next to Beth's body. She took a shuddering breath of grief. "I think this is where I should ask for my legal defense," she said.

"A public defender has been appointed for you, and

he will be visiting you shortly. But he and I -- and you -- know that there is no defense for what you've done. You have thumbed your nose at public authority, and even at holy Biblical law for American society. As a result of your rebellion, and your audacity in believing you are wiser than the dictates of Almighty God, a young woman is barely alive, and a precious baby is dead. Your friend Martha has been disbarred and disgraced; as we speak, she is being publicly flogged, and her punishment will be shown on tonight's newscast. Later today, she will be deported into exile on Judas Island. Your family are fugitives in Mormon territory. Oh, yes – we know that much: they crossed the mountains and were headed toward either Salt Lake City or Boise. You will never see them again. Never, Rachel."

Rachel bit her trembling lip, and willed herself to look into Cromwell's eyes. To her surprise, she saw a hint of softness there.

"Rachel, your sin has led to so much suffering...and I cannot understand how you, of all people, could commit such criminal acts. I know you are a good woman, with God indwelling. Can you explain this to me?"

His brow was knitted; he leaned slightly toward her.

"Magistrate...I am afraid to try," she said.

"Do not worry about saying anything that could be used against you in the trial," Cromwell said. "Nobody knows I am here, except the guard, whose loyalty I own completely. We are not being recorded, and nobody else can hear us. I have already stretched past the limits of accepted protocol to speak to you here today. Please talk to me. I may be able to offer you additional help, or I may be able to advise you as to how you and the public defender should best approach your case."

His eyes were still soft, his body language open, still leaning toward her slightly, as if eager to hear what she had to say. In her deeply intuitive way, she felt his own inner conflict, the pendulum swinging back and forth between sympathy for her, and outrage at what she had done. But his uncertainty meant there was indeed room for what she had to say. He might not accept it, but he would hear it, and that would have to be enough for now.

"Your eminence," she began, her rich voice gaining strength as she spoke. "Our new order seems in many ways to reflect the goodness which must be pleasing to God. We all experience more safety, and a more wholesome quality of life than our grandparents ever had. But, if you'll forgive my saying this – things could be better."

Cromwell sat back a bit. "Indeed, and how so? Our lives are safe and wholesome because we monitor obedience, and correct disobedience. Do you doubt that our doing so reflects the will of God?"

"No: I think that keeping peace and goodwill in the community is the will of God," Rachel replied.

"Do you question that conformity to the law is necessary, even paramount, for keeping that peace and goodwill, as you put it?"

She shook her head. "No. A Godly people must agree upon laws that protect the good of all, and must abide by them."

"Perhaps you doubt that your elders and leaders are acting faithfully in regard to the dictates of the Holy Bible?"

"No...I believe that their intentions are good and true."

Cromwell frowned. "Then what, Rachel, could we do to make things better?"

"Magistrate, now that I've had some jail time to ponder this...I respectfully submit to you that although the Holy Bible is sacred, our official interpretation of its divine dictates is flawed. I believe that the hearts and minds of those who are doing the interpretation are pure...but still, they are the hearts and minds of human beings, who are fallible."

"They are not fallible when they are teaching the literal and infallible truth of God's word," Cromwell said.

"Your Eminence, the Bible is inspired and holy. But human understanding may be flawed. There are passages in the Bible where interpretation cannot be avoided, and we humans, with different hearts and minds, and different life experiences, we are doomed to sometimes misinterpret. Two people, equally learned, equally pure, equally full of the love of God...well, sir, they can come to two different interpretations. There does not seem to me any infallibility in human understanding. I have come to the conclusion, recently, that sometimes our current government is flawed and in error in how it understands and enacts the word of God."

Cromwell took his glasses off and put them back on, as though doing so would clear his confusion. "Hmmmm. I must admit that I am amazed to hear this from you. I hardly know what to say."

Rachel looked at Cromwell, her gentle dark eyes luminous. "Magistrate...I am sorry for what I did, especially as it hurt those I love, and those I wanted to protect."

Their gazes locked for a long moment. "I believe you, Rachel," Cromwell said. "Your remorse, and your humility in admitting it, bode well for you." He glanced at his wristwatch. "I see that your public defender will soon arrive; I must be gone by then. Remember: we did not have this conversation."

Rachel nodded. He stood up, folded the chair under his arm, and left the cell. He took the key from his pocket, and she noticed that when he locked her in, he turned the key carefully and quietly. Perhaps it meant no more than that he did not want to draw attention to his presence, but she felt that after their conversation, he did not want to assault her with the unforgiving clash of steel on steel as the bolt slid to lock her in. She sat on her bunk, feeling the cold metal under her hands, wondering for a moment whether he had really been there, or if she had imagined the whole incident. But yes, he had been there – she could see the faint marks the rubber feet of the folding chair had made on the metal floor.

CHAPTER THIRTEEN

Soft regular electronic beeps, and the ever-present faint smell of disinfectant, greeted Nurse Abigail as she entered their very special patient's ICU room. Nurse Claire looked up from her painstaking task of cleaning and replacing a breathing tube. Abigail scrubbed her hands at the sink, and then went to look at their patient. Her arms were bruised from the IV lines, but her poor battered body had so many bruises and scrapes that it hardly mattered. She lay in the bed small and frail, looking almost like a newborn, with her head shaved, as had been required for examination and diagnosis after her terrible fall. But Abigail saw from the charts that the girl's vital signs were improving.

"Maybe this drug-induced coma is actually working – giving her body a chance to heal," Abigail said. "Maybe she really will pull through."

"If the Lord wills it," Claire said, laying her hand tenderly for a moment on their patient's head.

"And yet…how miserable for her, if she does." Abigail's tone was somber.

"Where there's life, there's hope," Claire reminded her. "Right?" she urged.

"Oh, of course, you're right. But I can't help wondering what hope that poor urchin ever had. You know?"

"I know." Claire watched the steady pulse of the heart monitor for a moment, the beats coming evenly and strong. "But if God saves her, the Lord must have a reason. Ours is not to reason why. Am I right?"

Abigail smiled. "Yeah. I'd like to see something better for this child."

"Me too. And maybe there will be something better for her...there seems to be a lot of interest in her." Claire turned to the printer, which was softly sliding out several sheets of paper. "How about you scan these reports over to the chief steward and the magistrate. Okay?"

Abigail took the printed reports from Claire. "Okay. And then I'll come back and read to her from the Bible for a while, like I did yesterday. I don't know if she can hear me, but – just in case she can, I'd like to."

Abigail turned to leave the room, thinking of what she would read to the fragile lost soul. *Psalms*, she thought. *The Lord is my shepherd; I shall not want.*

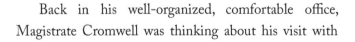

Back in his well-organized, comfortable office, Magistrate Cromwell was thinking about his visit with

Rachel, and about the upcoming trial. He had expected her to seem vulnerable and defeated, in the stark prison cell, but she hadn't been that way at all. Her sense of self, her goodness, were too strong to be dimmed by simple adverse circumstance. He thought of her doe-like eyes, her light-filled face. She was not just another criminal; he knew that. He knew it, but he had no choice other than to do his duty. The phone chimed. He saw that it was the Chief of Medicine at Penrose Hospital.

He pressed a button, and saw the man's worried face onscreen.

"Hello, Dr. Sutton," he said. "I received your electronic report. Thank you for taking the time to speak with me. I would like you to explain the report you sent."

"Magistrate, there is nothing to explain, sir," Dr. Sutton said. "The information I sent…that is what I know."

"So you are telling me that Bethany Laham's baby's DNA has been thoroughly compared to the entire national database of 'Y' chromosome samples, the samples mandatorily deposited by all living American males? You have run the comparisons twice, but you have not had a match? This is impossible, brother."

"Your Eminence, I cannot explain it. We have run the sample not only through our citizen database, but through the collection of registered visitors as well. We have made our request for collaboration through treaty to Canada and Mexico, and even the LDS territory has been asked for cooperation. As yet, no match has been discovered anywhere."

"I see," Cromwell said.

"And…Magistrate? No sample has been more than a 90% match. *That* is equally difficult to imagine. In fact, It is almost impossible to explain"

"Dr. Sutton, I simply don't know what to do with this information. I feel there must be something missing, or a mistake somewhere. I do not question your integrity; I believe there is something in this situation that is thus far eluding all of us. Please continue your diligent work, and keep me informed."

"Of course, Magistrate." Dr. Sutton hesitated. "There is one more thing, sir; that I must bring to your attention. The young woman who lost the baby…we ran her DNA as well, of course, as part of the process, and…well, sir, we discovered a very curious fact. Her DNA is an extremely close match with yours."

Cromwell's calm reply contradicted the suddenly wild beating of his heart. "Indeed? I trust you will recognize that at this juncture, that fact is irrelevant."

"Yes, Magistrate," Dr. Sutton agreed.

———⊙———

Two sets of footsteps echoed down the hallway again; Rachel looked up to see the guard, accompanied by a man who must be the public defender. Unsmiling, the guard unlocked the cell, locked him in with Rachel, and then handed him a pager. "Press this button when you want to leave," she said, and left them alone together.

Rachel was a bit surprised by the public defender; he was a short, stout man with a big round cherubic face. Hazel eyes twinkled merrily behind the small round-framed glasses. He seemed rather like a large elf, but he also carried himself with pride and confidence.

"Jared Irvine," he said, and extended a plump, well-manicured hand toward her.

"I'm glad to meet you," she said.

He sat down on the bunk next to her, and laid his briefcase on the floor.

"Reverend...your case is hopeless," he said, rather plainly. "But I have to tell you, I used to be good friends with Martha McIntosh, and I know a lot about you. I know so much about you and your work, you see, that I consider it an honor to stand up for you, even though I don't think we'll get anywhere." He smiled at her.

"Yes, Reverend, I would be willing to lose my own reputation and my career for the chance to defend you. You made mistakes, but by the God we both believe in, you made those mistakes with a pure heart. The tribunal won't care, but I do. I do, Reverend. It's our job to get up there and fight just as if we had a chance. And although we don't have a chance...the way we fight might make a difference in your sentencing."

Rachel remembered what Cromwell had said, that her sincere repentance boded well for her. She nodded, inviting Irvine to continue.

"The thing of it is, Reverend, that the quorum is dead set on making a public example of you. They have to, you see...you are so popular, and so well-thought-of, that if they don't, they run the risk of people imitating you, and then who knows what rebellion of charity and compassion they might have on their hands! So there will be a tribunal, and it will be televised, and my dear, you will be punished. The question that remains is to what degree you will be punished. There are some mitigating circumstances that we'll talk about, particularly in regard to your reputation and contributions to the community. But I think the strategy we should really think about is pleading no contention. Now, that doesn't mean I think you should get up there and say you're bad or wrong. We'll still say all we need to say – those are the extenuating circumstances. But it's clear that you broke the laws. You know that. Between you and me, maybe some of those laws were worth breaking. But we don't need to say that, not just yet. The point is that you did break the laws, and you know it. And if you're willing to say you know it...your sentence may be lighter. And I'd like to see that, Reverend, because I don't want to see you broken and your whole life lost to these mistakes."

Rachel nodded. "I'll think about it, Mr. Irvine."

"Good. We'll meet again briefly before the trial, and have a chance to go over final details then. I'll have a plan of action mapped out; I wanted to meet you first, to get a sense of how you'll appear to the tribunal, and what you're prepared to say."

Rachel smiled. "I have a lot to say, when the time is right," she said.

"I bet you do, Reverend; I bet you do."

"You were friends with Martha?" Rachel asked.

"I was. I think very highly of her. That's another reason why I asked to defend you. You have to be shown something...the law requires it...and I didn't want anyone else sitting here watching it with you."

"What...what are you talking about?" Rachel asked, confused.

All the light and levity faded from Mr. Irvine's amiable face. "Reverend, before you go before the tribunal, you have to watch a video recording of Martha McIntosh being caned in the town square. This is done to make you understand, really understand, both how your actions have caused others to suffer, and also the type of humiliation and chastisement you may face. I know you love Martha, and she loves you. I couldn't...well, I couldn't stand the thought of someone showing you this video who wasn't really on your side, who would maybe be curious about how you'd react. Because in the public defenders' office, there's not a lot of sentiment for you; you must know that."

"I...I don't really know much about it," Rachel admitted.

"Public sentiment is for you. The legal profession is against you. You flouted everything we stand for, and you hurt one of our own. Martha was well-respected, and now she's disgraced, disbarred. The public defenders – they're supposed to be impartial if they're assigned to a criminal, but nobody's ever really impartial about anything, not in their hearts. I figured it would be better for you, and for Martha, for you to have someone who's prejudiced in your favor. That's me, Reverend. I was the only one."

"I see." Rachel swallowed the lump in her throat. "What...do you have to show me?"

Irvine reached down and took a thin, flat computer from his briefcase. "The video's on here," he said. "Once it's shown, a signal will be sent back to the quorum that it's been seen."

"And it's of Martha?"

"Yes, Reverend. It's of Martha being caned this morning in the town square. Eight strokes."

There would never be a right time to see this video; she would never be ready, not as long as she lived. "Show me," she said.

He put the computer tablet in Rachel's lap, and pressed the power button. The screen was blank for a moment, and then she saw a camera panning across the town square. Everyone was there. They were packed so tightly that people could barely move. The crowd was quiet, except for an occasional cough, or the cry of a baby too young to be silenced. There was a raised wooden platform in the center of the square, which held a pillory. From the side of the screen, Martha came, wearing her prison uniform of gray pants and jacket. Her auburn hair was lifted off her neck in a tight bun. Her delicate-featured face seemed to have aged twenty years since Rachel last saw her. Her hands were shackled in front of her, and she was led, like a dog on a leash, by one of the stewards. He led her up to the pillory, and took off her jacket, leaving her wearing only a thin white blouse. He then transferred her hands into the manacles attached to the ironwork pillory. Then he bent her neck and locked her head into place. A low murmur ran through the crowd. Most of them had never seen a public caning; they were rare.

After a moment, Magistrate Cromwell strode onto the platform. Rachel could see the wintry unforgiving sky, and hard, small flakes of snow falling onto the shoulders of his suit. But he stood there without a coat, as if in some way he wanted to share Martha's discomfort.

"Martha McIntosh, for crimes against the state and against God, you have been sentenced to eight lashes, to be witnessed by our citizens, your peers, your brothers and sisters whom you have wronged in your defiance of the law," Cromwell said, his voice carrying surprisingly well across the square. "Vengeance belongs to the Lord; we take no satisfaction in the execution of this punishment. We ask God for mercy on you, and on all of us." He bowed his head for a moment, and then stepped off the platform.

Rachel did not know the man who stepped up behind Martha with the long, flexible rattan cane. He was some government official, she supposed. He raised his arm and struck Martha across her shoulders. The noise of the cane hitting her flesh echoed across the square. He waited several moments between strokes, so that she would feel each one fully, rather than being numb from pain. The eight strokes took only four minutes to complete, but it seemed like an eternity. Rachel heard and saw several people in the crowd bending over to vomit. When the final stroke was given, the man with the cane stepped back and bowed his head. The steward came and unlocked Martha's hands and head. She did not lift her face, but remained with her head bowed. The steward shackled her hands in front of her again and led her away, carrying her jacket over his arm. As she walked away, welts of blood showed clearly through her torn blouse. A mist of snow drifted down over the silently groaning crowd.

Irvine reached over and pressed another button, taking the computer tablet from Rachel. Tenderly, he wiped her tears from the screen with his handkerchief before he placed the tablet back into his briefcase.

"Martha will be loaded onto the next correctional train, on her way to exile on Judas Island," Irvine said softly, answering the question Rachel was too horrified to ask.

"What is Judas Island like?" Rachel forced herself to say.

"It's…rugged. Not the kind of place where anyone holds your hand, if you know what I mean. Ever read or heard any descriptions of that in-between place the old Catholics used to call Purgatory? That's the island…it's not quite hell, but you can see hell from there. Still, it is a second chance. It's probably better than execution."

"Yes…I suppose so." Rachel's heart felt as if it would break. She had brought such terrible suffering upon her beloved friend. "A place like that…it must change someone as kind as Martha."

Irvine nodded. "Yes, but not always in the way you think. Great tribulations harden some people, and others find strength they didn't know they had. You can't ever tell, until they get into the middle of it." He put his hand on Rachel's. "You're in the middle of it, Reverend. I can tell which type you'll turn out to be."

———— ((◉)) ————

CHAPTER FOURTEEN

The next day arrived, and in the few moments when Rachel was outside that Wednesday morning, the morning of her trial, as she was led from the jail to the transport van, and then the transport van to the courtroom, she felt a fierce gladness at the bitter cold weather and cascades of snow. The shock of the frigid air woke her up; the icy kiss of the snow on her cheek made her feel alive. She tried not to think too far ahead – there was no point in trying to anticipate what the tribunal would be like, or what would happen. But she felt ready.

She walked into the courtroom with as much grace as her shackled hands and feet would allow. The short chain between her ankles permitted only short steps, and she felt unbalanced, restrained as she was from moving her arms in a normal way. Her rubber-soled prison shoes made no noise on the black granite floor of the courtroom. All around her, there was nothing but cold stone, relieved only by wintry light from tall, small-paned windows. There was a gallery of black wooden benches for trials that were open to the public, but this one was not; it was too important that the visual and audio components of the tribunal be controlled, for it would be broadcast to an audience bound by law to watch, and it was important that the right impression be made. In their hasty consultation this morning prior to the trial, Irvine had told her that her shackles were also mostly for the benefit of the video-cast, although he had added, "Also, you might be a flight risk," and had nudged her very slightly with his elbow in a conspiratorial gesture, as if paying her the compliment of believing she had enough spirit to make a break for freedom.

The guard led Rachel to the defendant's station, where Irvine stood waiting for her. He nodded respectfully, and sat down next to her after she was seated. Only then did she look up at the judges' bench, which was in front of and above them, so that the judges looked down imperiously on the prisoner. Her heart sank when she saw that there were three judges. Cromwell was among them, impeccable and self-contained as always; he did not meet her eye. She wondered again whether she had somehow imagined his sympathetic visit the day before. One of the other two judges, who had straight black hair and dark skin, was younger than Cromwell, and therefore, paradoxically, more likely to be hard on her – he had never known any regime other than the theocracy in which they now lived, and his generation believed in it unquestioningly. The third judge was old enough to be Cromwell's father;

his long wrinkled face, set into somber lines, looked the most unforgiving of the three.

But he stood up readily, without even the aid of a cane. "For the purpose of the future video-cast of this trial, I will introduce the parties present. Defendant Rachel DeLine is represented by defense attorney Jared Irvine. Sitting in judgment for the state and for God, I am the Right Honorable Judge Samuel Bartlett; to my right is Magistrate Jerry Cromwell, and to his right is Elder Franklin Summers. The collective judgment of the statutes of law, civic practice, and church law will be given today as we sentence Rachel DeLine. Elder Summers, please continue." And with that, the elderly judge sat down.

Summers stood. "The purpose of this trial is to demonstrate the futility and folly of insubordination against heavenly law. We will be inspired by dominance of the order of the triumphal over chaos. Once again, the absolute control of God's righteous law will restore justice. The example of disobedience will draw unto itself the natural consequences incurred in rebellion against God's order.

"This offender – this perpetrator of subversive acts against our holy order – stands accused on five counts." As he spoke, a screen descended from the ceiling above the judges, and the accusations appeared in bold black script as he read them. Rachel was glad she had heard them before, both from Cromwell and from Irvine. It would have been shocking to hear them and see them for the first time now, in these bleak surroundings.

"One: Failure to report a crime. Two: Harboring a fugitive from the law. Three: Aiding and abetting a fugitive. Four: Evading and resisting arrest. Five: Accessory to third-degree murder." Summers paused for a moment, allowing the gravity of the charges to sink in – again for the benefit of the video audience. "We will show the facts of her mutinous contempt for divine law, and her attempt to evade justice. And finally, we will show that she is ultimately guilty of contributing to the delinquency of a juvenile, and inciting a reckless hazard that led to manslaughter.

"When the offender's guilt is clearly established, the verdict will be obvious. It is obvious even now, but as a civilized society, we insist upon following the correct protocol. Since there can be no defense against these charges, a confession would be a matter for consideration when this tribunal deliberates regarding sentencing. The offender will testify. Any refusal to answer will be deemed an admission of guilt. Would the defendant care to confess?" Summers stared at Rachel, his dark eyes hard as flint.

Irvine stood up. Suddenly his round face no longer looked so cherubic and innocent, and his confidence magnified into a poise that drew the judges' attention to him with respectful interest. "Your Honors," Irvine said, "on the advice of counsel, my client would offer a partial confession in the form of a no-contention plea to the first four charges against her. We feel that the matter of the fifth charge has facets that are disputable, and must be contended; we intend to request that the prosecution drop that charge. If not, we will present our defense."

The three judges huddled together for a moment, murmuring. Then they all nodded. Summers addressed Irvine: "You must realize that the charge of manslaughter is the most serious of the crimes laid to your client's account. The gravity of this entire proceeding is based upon the fact that your client's confessed actions resulted in the loss of one life, and another still hanging in the balance. Therefore, your request for a plea bargain is denied. I must warn you and your client not to try the patience of this tribunal. We intend to see a swift deliverance of justice, not chaos. Do I make myself clear, Counselor?"

"Perfectly clear, Your Honor," Irvine replied.

"Very well, then. I will leave it to my esteemed colleague, Justice Bartlett, to present the facts against your client."

Rachel raised her eyes bravely to the judges as they read the facts against her. As with the charges, the information was printed on the screen above the judges. As the list of her transgressions grew longer and longer, Rachel began to lose all hope of anything other than a death sentence. Quietly she admitted to each of the condemning facts presented. They were all true, on the surface, though presented in stark black and white, none of them showed what had been in her heart. She dreaded the presentation of the fifth charge…it would be very difficult for her to admit guilt to the court. She had never intended to endanger Beth or her child – in fact, everything she had done had been with exactly the opposite intent: to protect them. She felt her stomach churning with apprehension as the discussion of the fourth charge drew to a close, and she clenched her teeth, trying to steel herself.

Suddenly, to her surprise, Cromwell rose. "My fellow judges, you will note that we have been in session for nearly three hours. I observe that the defendant is pale, and looks faint. While it is our intention to visit justice upon her, it is not our intention to be cruel. I move that we adjourn for half an hour, and that the defendant be permitted to rest and collect herself in chambers. We would all benefit, I think, from the opportunity to take a breath."

"Well said, Magistrate," agreed Judge Bartlett, who was looking tired and strained himself.

"Your mercy does you credit," Elder Summers said.

Cromwell nodded briefly. "Guard, take the defendant and her counsel to the judges' chambers."

Rachel almost protested – could they not simply get this terrible proceeding over with? But Irvine discreetly squeezed her hand; he sensed that there was more to this than met the eye. Before putting her in chambers, the guard accompanied Rachel to the women's restroom, where she relieved herself and splashed a little cold water on her face. Then she was led to chambers, which was a more comfortable room than the courtroom. The guard stood outside the door, while Rachel and Irvine sat together, not speaking.

"Just take these moments to rest your mind, if you can," Irvine suggested. "I know this last charge will be the hardest for you to endure. But it seems that pleading guilty is your best chance."

"They are going to condemn me to death," Rachel said, her voice flat.

"You don't know that," Irvine reprimanded her.

"Yes, I do. I'm sure of it," Rachel whispered.

They were surprised when a panel in the wall behind the desk opened – it was a hidden door that led from chambers to the courtroom, so that the judges could go back and forth without being troubled by the public. Cromwell came in, and stood in front of them.

"Stay seated," he said, as Irvine started to rise. "I haven't much time. But I want to urge you to present any and all mitigating or even exculpatory evidence in answer to the charge of manslaughter." He reached into his pocket, and gave Irvine a small card. "I know this is unexpected, and you have very little time to prepare. Those are points you might consider making. My intention is to counsel leniency when my colleagues and I are in the sentencing process."

"But…we were told that the best chance for Reverend

DeLine was to plead guilty," Irvine said.

Cromwell shook his head. "The other judges do not know this case as well as I do," he said. "I know you must suspect my motives in advising you this way. I can only ask that you take the risk of trusting me. If anyone knew I was here, speaking to you…well, you can imagine what the consequences would be. I am taking as great a risk as the one I am suggesting to you. Tell the court about Rachel DeLine, Counselor Irvine. You will not be denying the charge – you will merely be telling the whole story. I must go – may God bless you."

And with that, he turned and disappeared through the same panel in the wall.

"What…" Irvine began.

"Go ahead and do as he suggests," Rachel said. Between this and the mysterious visit yesterday, she knew that somehow, in some way, Cromwell was at least partly on her side. "I think we can trust him."

<hr/>

Cromwell stood outside on the courthouse steps, taking deep breaths of cold air. In his mind's eye, he saw a young woman…a woman who looked like him, with slightly ascetic, regular features, and large mist-grey eyes. Ruth. Ruth, his much younger sister. Poor Ruth…an unexpected child, late in their parents' life, who had not been given the benefit of as much attention and guidance as he'd had from them. Sixteen years ago, she had disappeared. Nobody knew why, but everyone suspected that she was illegally pregnant. She had never really fit in, never really conformed. He suspected that she had left her baby, Bethany Marie Laham, at the orphanage. Bethany had been their great-grandmother's name. And how else could Beth be such a close DNA match? It made so much sense, and it was so tragic.

He realized that Ruth had seen only one side of him: the side that despised weakness and loved order and righteousness. She had not seen the tenderness he had toward the innocent and vulnerable. He had to admit to himself that if she had told him of her trouble, he would have judged her, even though he loved her. But he and his wife would have sheltered and loved her child. His niece, his lost, unloved niece…he felt that he might have had a hand in her misfortunes, by not being a more openly loving brother to Ruth. Of course, all of this was conjecture. He shook his head, trying to clear it. There was very little evidence that he and Bethany Laham were possibly related. Not any actual proof, at all. And yet…Rachel had risked everything for this girl, this stranger. Rachel had risked all: perhaps because his sister had not trusted him in her time of need. And the Laham girl looked very much like Ruth. He couldn't get away from that thought.

———— ((●)) ————

In order to protect Cromwell, Rachel was careful not to let her body language change when the tribunal reconvened. Irvine had spent the remainder of the recess making notes, going over his arguments under his breath, completely absorbed in deciding what he should say. She trusted him, so she allowed herself to relax for those few moments, taking comfort in prayer. She no longer felt that she would be executed; Cromwell was a powerful and persuasive man, and if he were on her side, she would come out of this trial with her life. In order to keep him on her side, she knew she must not betray his support in any way. So she sat with her head bowed as Judge Bartlett presented the bleak facts of the fifth and final charge against her, agreeing meekly to each fact as it was printed on the screen above the bench.

The charge was presented cleverly, in such a way as to make it inarguable. Her motivation was never brought up; they discussed only the indisputable facts. If Rachel had not encouraged Beth to avoid arrest, Beth would not have fled. If Beth had not fled, she would not have gone into hazardous territory. If she had not gone into hazardous territory, she would not have fallen…and the fall caused her miscarriage. The miscarriage led in a straight line back to Rachel, and her string of unlawful decisions. Even if

Beth recovered from her injuries, the advanced medical care she had required as a result of the accident had been a significant burden to the state.

When Judge Bartlett had finished his presentation, his cracked old voice strained from talking so long, Jared Irvine stood. "Your Honors, Rachel DeLine does not contest the facts of these charges. However, in the matter of sentencing, as her counsel, I would like to present, on her behalf, certain mitigating circumstances. I want to emphasize that Rachel DeLine has not encouraged me to do this. As her defense counsel, it is my job to see the situation more objectively than she herself is able to do. And as someone well-acquainted with this case, and with her history, I strongly feel that there are facets of her character and life that should be taken into consideration when you decide how she should be punished."

"Very well, Counselor," Elder Summers said. "You may continue."

"Thank you," Irvine said. He looked from one face to the next on the judges' bench, his twinkling eyes now somber. "I don't deny to this court that Rachel DeLine made errors of judgment. But I do want to say this: that they were errors of judgment, not premeditated acts of rebellion against holy law. The dilemma Rachel encountered was unlike anything she had ever seen before. As a woman who had dedicated her life to helping mothers and children, it's to be expected that her heart would go

out to Bethany Laham, still a child herself, who showed
up in such desperate trouble. Rachel's record of conduct
has been impeccable; her ministry center has complied
with every aspect of the law, and has often been used as an
example, in our community and beyond, as a model of efficiency and compassion. She herself has a spotless record
as a law-abiding citizen, as does her husband. There has
never been so much as a complaint against her.

"This isn't a woman who was prone to subverting the
law; nor had she any plans to rebel. This is a woman who
lived all her life in compliance, and who worked to better
the lives of others. In an exceptional situation, she allowed
her heart to rule her head. But even then, she tried to
do what was right; she sought legal advice from Martha
McIntosh, now convicted and exiled. Rachel DeLine is
deeply loyal to her friend, and has not told me what advice
she was given. But I would point to the fact of Martha
McIntosh's being an accessory to this crime as evidence
that the situation was highly unusual and confusing. Mrs.
McIntosh also had a prior spotless reputation; she was
one of the finest lawyers in our region. And even she, Your
Honors, couldn't see clearly when presented with the case
of Bethany Laham.

"Rachel DeLine was ordained a minister of the
Gospel. As of now, she still holds the title of Reverend.
Her community loves and respects her, and with good
reason. I would humbly suggest to the court that Rachel

has work still to do in this world, and on behalf of Rachel and the people whose lives she has touched, I ask you to give her an appropriate penance that will allow her, still, to give of herself to those around her. Rachel DeLine's crime was one of love misplaced, not of deliberate wickedness. Allow her, please, to keep using that love of people and love of God in a way that can redeem her mistakes. I thank the court for hearing me."

Irvine bowed his head, and sat down. Rachel could see sweat beading at his temples. She was moved by what he had said, and amazed at how skillfully he had walked the line between acknowledging her guilt and asking for mercy. It remained to be seen what the judges would do.

"Rachel DeLine," Judge Bartlett said, "the tribunal has convicted you of all five charges against you, to which you have wisely pleaded no contest. We will recess until tomorrow, when you will be required to speak before you are sentenced. I will remind you of the rules of court: you may say whatever you wish; as long as you remain civil, you do not blaspheme, and you offer no contempt of court, you may speak without interruption. I need hardly remind you that what you say may have a significant impact, for good or ill, on your sentence. You have until tomorrow to think carefully about what you wish to say. Court is adjourned!"

Rachel found that she was almost too exhausted to stand. Irvine gently supported her as she stumbled out of the courtroom. "Do you want me to help you decide what to say tomorrow?" he asked.

She shook her head. "No. I have to say what's in my heart, and I will trust that when the time comes, I'll know what's right. I can only tell the truth, and that will have to be enough. I am so grateful to you, Mr. Irvine."

He smiled. "As I've said before, Reverend, it's an honor to be here with you. There is no disgrace in this…in being accused of crimes, and to be on trial. Many of the sacred heroes of our faith found themselves in just this situation. Even our Lord Jesus demonstrated that some laws deserve to be broken. You are in good company, Rachel. There's not much more I can do…except this." He rummaged in his briefcase for a moment, and took out a bar of rich dark chocolate. "I hear this is your special weakness," he said. "I thought it might make a nice change from prison food."

She took it from him, and slipped it inside the pocket of her drab prison pants. "Mr. Irvine, you always know exactly the right thing to do," she said.

Late that night as Rachel lay on her hard metal bed, she treated herself to a square of the chocolate, thinking about Martha, and Irvine, and Cromwell, and her husband…the people who were still supporting her, some of them in very unexpected ways. Whatever happened at the trial, she couldn't let them down. Whatever life was left to her, she would continue to live it with all the faith and strength God would give her.

———— ➤((◉))◄ ————

Nurse Abigail's eyes widened when she saw Magistrate Cromwell standing outside Beth's ICU room, watching from a distance, silent. She went over to the door, carrying Beth's chart.

"Magistrate, it's so kind of you to visit in person," she said. "You'll be glad to know that Miss Laham is doing much better. There's no question that she will live, though she'll need care for a while yet."

"I saw from the electronic records that she has been brought out of the drug-induced coma," Cromwell said, his eyes not on Abigail, but on the fragile young woman in the bed.

"Yes – and we're so pleased; she's breathing well on her own, and everything is working as it should. The coma allowed her body to let go of the trauma from the accident, and concentrate on healing itself. She couldn't feel any pain or distress, which helped greatly in her healing." She offered the chart to Cromwell so that he could see for himself, but he did not take it.

"Is she…has she spoken at all?"

"She has been conscious for brief periods, but we're trying to keep her quiet. There can't be any good in her asking a lot of questions right now."

"Does she know that she lost the baby?"

"I don't know, Magistrate. We haven't spoken of it. We don't want to distress her by talking about it until and unless she is ready."

Cromwell nodded. "That seems wise." He smiled briefly at Abigail, but again, his attention was distracted toward Beth.

"Nurse, would you allow me a few moments alone with her? As you can imagine, involved as I am in the trial of Reverend DeLine, the recovery of this young girl is much on my mind. I would simply like to sit with her, and pray. I give you my word that should she waken, I will not say anything to distress or trouble her."

"Of course, Magistrate," Abigail said. "It's unlikely that she'll wake up, so don't worry too much about that. She was awake a little while ago, and just being conscious for a few minutes tires her out, poor soul. I can update the electronic chart while you're with her."

"Thank you, Nurse," Cromwell said, hiding his impatience for her to leave. Finally she walked away down the hall, and he was alone with Beth, and his own thoughts. He walked into the ICU room, wrinkling his nose slightly at the antiseptic smell. He sat down in the vinyl-covered chair near the bed, and looked at Beth's face, still slightly swollen and discolored from the bruises caused by her fall. Even with her shaved head, he couldn't help seeing the Cromwell family features in her face. She was tiny, like a bird, just as Ruth had been. What had become of Ruth?

He would probably never know.

Rachel firmly believed the girl's story that she had become pregnant although she was a virgin. No match had been found for the baby's DNA. How was this possible? Nothing in medical science could account for it… but then, nothing in medical science could explain the miraculous pregnancy of the Virgin Mary. Christian history, and faith in God, promoted the possibility that a virgin could conceive. But that had been about the birth of the Messiah – if Beth's story were true, the implications would be earth-shattering. And the fact that the baby had been lost…well, that was too much to contemplate. Surely if the child had been conceived by some divine intervention, it would also have been saved by God? And yet, God never took away free will – so, in fact, some decisions and events unfolded against the Will of God. If Mary and Joseph had not fled King Herod, perhaps Jesus would not have survived to the age of three! But, Mary and Joseph chose to heed a warning, and to flee. Beth's choice had resulted in tragedy. If her child had been miraculous, she would still have had free will. But her pregnancy couldn't possibly be a miracle – could it?

Tired from his day in court, Cromwell put his head in his hands for a moment to stop the dizzy swirl of his thoughts. Educated though he was, prayerful as he was, confident he surely was in his understanding of holy law, yet he could not make sense of Beth's pregnancy. But with every passing minute, he was more certain that she *was* his niece. That, in itself, was a miracle.

He sat quietly with Beth for an hour, praying for her, and praying for guidance in the upcoming sentencing of Rachel DeLine.

CHAPTER FIFTEEN

The following day was still cold and snowy, but Rachel felt a warmth inside her as she was led to the courtroom. To her own surprise, she had been able to sleep the night before, and she had fallen asleep feeling as though she were being held in the loving embrace of all the people who believed in her. Today was her day to speak, but she hadn't spent much time thinking about what to say. She meant what she had said to Irvine, that her heart and the Spirit would speak through her, if she were open and ready to be a channel for the truth she carried within her. It wouldn't be easy, but she had no doubt that she was ready to speak her truth.

The guard led her into the courtroom and seated her next to Irvine again. The three judges were already assembled, waiting for her. After giving her a moment to collect herself, Elder Summers rose and said: "Reverend Rachel DeLine, before this court convenes to determine your sentence for the five criminal charges to which you have pleaded no contest, we invite you to address us. We are not inviting a defense; there is, as we have determined, no defense for your actions. We invite you to provide us with insight as to your character, so that we are better able to devise a sentence suited to you and to the community you have wronged." He sat down again, and stared at Rachel with his flinty eyes.

Carefully, aware that her legs were shaking with fear, Rachel stood. She looked into the eyes of each judge: the uncompromising dark eyes of Elder Summers, the slate-blue eyes of Judge Bartlett; and finally she looked into Cromwell's large grey eyes. There was the faintest trace of a smile in his eyes, just the briefest flash, and she took courage. She took a deep breath, inhaling to the inwardly spoken words "Merciful Christ," and exhaling to the words "Sustain me." She felt able to speak, but she still trembled like an aspen in the wind.

As she began to speak, she mentally addressed herself to Cromwell, though she was careful not to look only at him, for fear that the other two judges would guess that he had given her some special encouragement. But her words were all for him. Her deep, rich voice rang clearly through the cold stone courtroom, sweet as a bell, despite her nerves.

"As this learned assembly is no doubt aware, William Shakespeare, in his play *The Merchant of Venice*, created a scene in which the character of Portia speaks a famous line to the character of Shylock, who is very big on law and order. She says: 'In the course of *real justice*, **none** of us should ever see salvation.' In other words, if any of us were going to get what we truly deserve in God's judgment, then we would all be doomed.

"But, if it please this court, I do not believe in doom. I believe in the mercy of Christ, and in our Lord's amazing grace. I stand here today in the conviction of my Christian faith that law – even Biblical law – is incapable of giving salvation, and that only *love* can save any of us. Humbly, I submit that this is not my original thought; I take this from the great apostle of Christ, Saint Paul. In First Corinthians, Chapter 9, Saint Paul writes that he cannot be made right with God through obedience to the law… only faith in God will do that. He says that he is now ***dead to the law***, and alive to God through his relationship with Jesus.

"And what of our Lord? Jesus teaches us that God, our Savior, is like a father who keeps hoping for the return of the prodigal, and when he sees that one from afar, he does not stand on propriety – rather, he runs without dignity to embrace the repentant one who returns. Jesus wants us to know that God is like that! God does not scapegoat; nor does God condemn anyone…at any time, for any transgression.

"Your Honors, based on my upbringing in the Christian faith, I respectfully submit to you that justice is getting what we deserve…but ***mercy*** - well, mercy is getting what we do ***not*** deserve. And grace, which is what

God offers us again and again in scripture, is **getting better than we deserve**. Grace trumps all law.

"Take, for example, the case of Mother Mary, when she was a teenaged maiden in Nazareth. When she was engaged to Joseph, but before they were married, when by law she was required to be a pure virgin – she was found to be with child! This was a violation of Mosaic Law, and a capital crime, one that called for death by stoning. And yet, amazing grace prevailed. Joseph listened to the message from God that he should *ignore the law.* Yes, that's right – it was *God's decision* that an *exception* to the law was just and holy, *if* it were for the sake of compassionate love that could save a soul. A young, unwed woman, who was found to be with child – although nobody could explain how that had happened – was **not** subject to the strictures of Divine Law.

"Ooh, is it any wonder justice wears a blindfold?! The blindfold hides her tears at the tragic miscarriages of justice visited upon the young and ignorant, who are sacrificed merely to purge the sins of the old and wicked…so that we who should know better will vainly attempt to attain a purity that can *never, never* be ours!

"I remain convinced that the young woman I befriended was no different from the Virgin Mary. She was good and innocent – and, I believe, she was a pure virgin. How did she become pregnant? I don't know; but then again, no one else has figured that out, either! Have you?!

And yet, our law is set to pre-judge her, to condemn her as guilty of a crime that cannot be proven. We are supposedly believers in the mysterious and even 'the inscrutable ways of God,' as Saint Paul called them – and yet, who among you has even noticed how her name reminds us of the Virgin Mother of Christ? Beth Laham…Bethlehem?

"Well, I have said too much, I suppose. My friends and family will tell you that's an unfortunate habit of mine. So I will conclude by asking you to consider the greatest commandment of our Lord and Savior, Jesus Christ: 'That you love.' That is all righteousness. And, he has told us that *all* the Law and the Prophets hang on this! Just love, he commands us; love our God, and love our neighbors as we love ourselves. That is all I have to say. I thank the Court for its kind attention."

No longer shaking, Rachel bowed her head and sat down. There was a long silence before Cromwell banged the gavel, and announced that the judges would retire to chambers to discuss the sentence.

CHAPTER SIXTEEN

After two hours of discussion in chambers, the three judges looked exhausted. Although not all of them wanted to admit it, Rachel DeLine's speech had struck all of them, in different ways. Judge Bartlett, the eldest of the three, remembered a time before theocracy when "liberal" Christian viewpoints had echoed many of the points Rachel had just made. Elder Summers, who had grown up in theocratic America, was disturbed by some of the points she had made, which in good conscience he could not agree with, but which pointed out inconsistencies between Jesus' teachings and this government's methods of dealing with people. And Magistrate Cromwell, though outwardly calm, felt a growing knot in his gut as he argued, as dispassionately as possible, for leniency in Rachel's case. It was imperative that the other judges not know he had any personal stake in the outcome. His self-control was extraordinary, but it was harder and harder not to betray his feelings.

"Gentlemen," he said, "I know, from our discussion here, that the case of Rachel DeLine has struck all of us as unusual. We have laid out, several times, the facts against her, and have weighed those facts against the traditional sentencing guidelines. We all know that if we go by the book, Rachel DeLine will be sentenced to death. And yet, the fact that we are still deliberating here would suggest that none of us feels this to be the correct protocol in her case. Am I correct?" He gestured obliquely at the litter of papers on the table, which bore witness to their agonized calculations.

Summers and Bartlett both nodded. Of the three men, Cromwell seemed to have the most energy left, and they were willing to let him speak. Cromwell adjusted his steel-rimmed glasses, and made clear, commanding eye contact with his fellow-judges.

"Very well, then. Misguided though this young woman is, and questionable though her closing speech may in some ways have been – from my perspective, the overriding factor in this case is that Mrs. DeLine can still be redeemed. Her motivation in helping Bethany Laham was not a deliberate rebellion against the government; her heart overrode her head. If she is unsupervised in general society, this trait is dangerous to us all. But on the penal colony of Judas Island, she could do a great deal of good among her fellow-prisoners. We are all aware of the criticisms we receive from domestic and foreign governments regarding Judas Island; though I do not think the conditions there compare in any way to the prisoner of war camps to which the island is often compared. It is irrefutable that the colony suffers from a lack of morale. The exiled prisoners often die prematurely, and even while they are there, they regularly fail to perform assigned tasks with efficiency or dedication.

"But, I believe that the presence of Rachel DeLine on Judas Island could cause a great deal of positive change that might reflect well on our government. Both of you have mentioned your concerns that although she has admitted her guilt, her spirit is not broken. Again, I say – in the general population that would represent a danger. But on Judas Island, it is of benefit to us. Helping people is the wellspring of this woman's nature. I move that we allow her to do what she is driven to do, in a controlled penal colony environment where she can do our country no harm."

Bartlett and Summers considered this. "But she must do public penance," Summers argued.

"Let her be flogged in the public square, as Martha McIntosh was," Cromwell suggested. "Remember that this penance carries different weight for different criminals. For a woman as proud as Rachel is, to be whipped in front of her peers is perhaps a worse sentence than to simply die with dignity. Most of the criminals sentenced to flogging are already broken in spirit, and no longer care what is done to them. Flogging, for Mrs. DeLine, is a proportionately difficult burden, and a worthwhile penalty."

Bartlett nodded. "I take your point, Cromwell, and I am inclined to agree."

Summers said, "But we must show clearly that her actions were not in any way sanctioned by our society. She must be stripped of her theological credentials – she must be defrocked."

Cromwell smiled to himself – this nod to official protocol would hardly be an embarrassment, when the law itself was due to "defrock" Rachel soon anyway. But, if this meaningless gesture pacified Elder Summers so much the better.

"I agree," he said. "She must be seen to have all authority taken from her."

"But it seems that this sentence is no different from what happened to her friend, Martha McIntosh," Summers fretted. "Yet her crime was greater."

Cromwell shook his head. "The sentence, while the same, has more impact on Rachel DeLine," he said. "Martha McIntosh was a good lawyer, but her heart was not in her work in the same way that Rachel's is in hers. Martha betrayed her job in a way that Rachel does not believe she has betrayed hers. Stripping Rachel of her title means something different to her. Do you see?"

Summers rubbed his forehead to ease the crease of worry between his brows. "I do see, Magistrate," he admitted. "And I also see the danger of too strict a punishment. There is a great deal of public sentiment in support of

Rachel DeLine."

"If we martyr her…we do so at our peril," Cromwell finished the rationale for him. He knew that there was already some worry about public response to Rachel's sentencing; the quorum of elders had decided, for this reason, that it should not be televised live.

The three men nodded. They were agreed, but only Cromwell had victory singing in his heart.

⸺((◉))⸺

Rachel looked around her barren stainless-steel cage. Shortly she would be taken from it, and sent away to a fate that was far better than the fears that had haunted her dreams. But still, her punishment would be harsh. In her mind's eye, she played again and again the vision of Martha being caned. Would she herself be able to endure without bawling or wailing? She hoped so, but she was afraid. And she was afraid of what awaited her on Judas Island. Still – Martha would be there. Rachel took comfort in this thought.

She heard a set of footsteps approaching down the echoing hallway. Looking up, she recognized the solid, immaculate figure of Magistrate Cromwell. He did not speak as he arrived at her cell, but silently unlocked the door, entered, and locked the door again behind him. This time he had not brought his folding chair.

Rachel stood up. "Magistrate," she said. "I'm surprised to see you." She gestured to her hard metal bed. "Would you like to sit down?"

He hesitated for a moment, but then accepted her invitation. She sat next to him. "You were right," she said. "The tribunal did not condemn me to death." She wanted to tell him that she knew she owned him her life, but she did not quite dare. "I've been told that in the next hour or so, I will go to be f-flogged—" her voice cracked on the word "—in the public square, and then I will be put on a train to permanent exile on Judas Island. And to think, when we met a week ago, I was worried only about losing my job at the ministry center!"

"It has been a week of extraordinary events," Cromwell replied. "And I am saddened that it has come to this. You may not believe me, but none of this gives me the least satisfaction…in fact, quite the opposite. I find myself more deeply disturbed than I could have imagined - just a week ago - when our troubles began."

He stopped abruptly, took his glasses off, and polished them with his handkerchief. Rachel watched him carefully. She gently asked, "May I ask…why you are disturbed, sir?"

Cromwell smiled to himself. She was not asking because she was curious; once again, he was struck by the genuine compassion for her fellow human beings that rose up in her, no matter what the circumstance. She saw that he was hurting, and she wanted to share his burden. Her sincerity resonated in her deep, clear voice.

"Rachel…I do not know how to tell you this, but I am deeply indebted to you." He put his glasses back on, more comfortable behind their familiar shield. "You have saved my niece – a niece I never knew existed." Rachel's brow knitted with confusion, as he continued. "My dear sister, whom I deeply cherished…she disappeared, many years ago, and it now seems that she ran away from the family when she was…when she found herself with an unplanned, illegal pregnancy. It would seem she abandoned her baby girl at the door of the orphanage, with a note that said the child's name was 'Bethany Marie Laham.'"

Rachel gasped in amazement, her eyes open wide.

Cromwell went on. "You have said so many things that I ponder – yes, I really do – but what strikes me most deeply is your belief that God brought Beth to you. I think…I mean to say, it made me feel…somehow, a sense of reality - deep reality. It…I felt it like a chord of music played in my soul. Do you know that feeling, Rachel?" She nodded. "I could not allow you to be taken away without having a chance to say this to you…that maybe you were right about God bringing Beth to you." He took a deep breath, and let it out slowly. "I am a logical man, Rachel, and I see that if I am willing to say you may have been right about that, then it follows that the Holy Spirit may have given you revelation about other things – matters that I will continue to ponder, for a long, long time after today. That is what I wanted you to know."

He nodded politely to her, and stood up, preparing to leave. She gathered her courage. "Magistrate?"

He turned back toward her. "Yes?"

"Now that I am in no position to share the knowledge with anyone – I wonder if you could tell me about the black vans that take unwed, pregnant young women away? I know I am still not cleared for such classified information, but – what harm could it do for me to know - now?"

Cromwell paused, and put the key back in his pocket. "Oh, that. Well, Rachel, those girls are taken to what we call a 'baby farm,' where they are given expert medical care. They are clothed, fed, and housed, and they deliver their babies in a hospital. The babies are allowed to breast feed and bond with the mothers, so that they will feel loved and secure. During this time, the staff looks for adoptive parents for the child. Ideally, a baby goes directly to an adoptive couple once it is no longer breastfeeding. Sometimes the babies go to an orphanage, but that happens less and less – it has always been one of my personal goals to have as low a ratio as possible of orphanage babies, and I must say, this experience with Bethany Laham has reinforced my dedication to *that* cause. Eventually the mothers are exiled to Judas Island. Occasionally, if a woman comes to us who has exceptional gifts with babies, or with other women, we keep her as staff."

"Oh," Rachel said, surprised. "That isn't as bad as what people imagine, when they see women crying and screaming, hauled into those vans and driven off to who knows where. It scares people to see that. Although…well, it seems to me that trying to scare people into obedience is what our law system really amounts to."

"Hmmm," Cromwell said, neither agreeing nor disagreeing. "You do not seem to know much of fear, yourself."

Rachel's smile was tremulous, her mouth quivering with emotion held in check. She said, "Oh no, Magistrate! You are wrong about that! I was terrified when I addressed the tribunal, and I have been so frightened today. I thought I would lose my mind with fear; it was such a relief to see you, and speak to you…another person, someone just to remind me that I'm still in the real world. My heart aches for my daughter and husband; being without them is like losing a vital part of my own body. And I know I will have to endure that loss for…God only knows how long! I am afraid for them, especially my daughter…afraid that she thinks I abandoned her, afraid of how she will grow up without me. John is the best father in the world, but it's not the same as having a mother, especially for a little girl.

"I am afraid of the pain of flogging, especially after watching Martha go through it. I am afraid of Judas Island, especially after what Jared Levine told me about it. I am even scared of the future that is not my own – afraid of the what will go on in this Christian nation, which still has people in it that I care about…Beth, and you, my friends and family, and everyone I've ever met through my ministry. Maybe when I confess my fear, I betray a lack of faith in our Lord and Savior. But all of this is to say – I *do* know fear, Magistrate! It haunts me all the time."

Cromwell had not missed the fact of his being included in the list of people she cared about, and feared for. It had *not* been calculated for effect. Her generosity of spirit humbled him. For a moment, he was tempted to tell her of what he hoped to do for Beth, but that *would* have been calculated…and it would endanger both of them, at this point, were she to know. He would have liked to demonstrate to Rachel how meeting her had genuinely changed him. But it would not be appropriate, and it would not be safe.

Instead, he said, "You are understandably under an almost unbearable strain right now, Rachel. But I can tell you this: fear does not contradict faith. Faith allows you to carry on and do what is right even in the face of fear. And I know that your faith is awe-inspiring. Goodbye, Rachel."

She could not bear to watch him go. She heard the bolt slide to unlock the door, and heard its cold metal thud as it locked again. As Cromwell's footsteps echoed away down the corridor, she had never felt so alone. She heard his words repeating themselves in her mind: *Faith allows you to carry on and do what is right in the face of fear.* She knew what she must do now. Difficult though it was to shift her focus from herself, she closed her eyes, stilled her mind, quieted her breathing, and began to pray: for her family, for Martha, for Beth, for all those whom she had accidentally hurt or endangered, for her community, for the world. She did not presume to ask the God she loved for anything specific; to do so would have been to suggest that she knew best. But she prayed for grace, and mercy, and guidance for all of them. And she thanked God that she had been granted the gift of life, and she asked to be shown how to use her life in his service. As she prayed, she felt a sense of renewed hope. She could go on.

⚫

CHAPTER SEVENTEEN

J ohn DeLine spread the creased map over the orange
Formica tabletop, obliquely watching his daughter out of the corner of his eye as she fed bits of tuna to
Esmeralda through the door of her cat carrier. The small
family-owned deli adjacent to the auto service center had
been nice enough to let them bring the cat carrier inside
while the McIntosh sedan was being serviced. After the
long drive to their current location near Spokane, Washington, John wanted to make sure the car was in prime
condition before the next leg of the trip. He could tell
that the long hours of sitting in the car were hard on both
Odie and Maggie, but there was no help for it. Soon they
would be able to relax a little, but for now, they had to
remain on the move.

"We could stay for a while with my nephew – he and
his family live near Davenport," Odie suggested, pushing
her turkey sandwich aside.

"Maybe, but only temporarily, until I can find work
out on the coast… somewhere on the Olympic Peninsula;
maybe in Port Angeles, or Sequim. From there, it will be

easier for us to seek full emigration to Vancouver, and that is the most important thing. We need full Canadian passports in order to safely pursue visitation rights to Judas Island, without worrying about being kept there. We need the protection of the Canadian government."

He took another sip of watery coffee, and sighed. Maggie looked up at him with her big dark eyes, so much like her mother's. She had her mother's natural candor, too, and she asked, "Why would you want to go there, Daddy? It's a bad, scary place!"

"You're right, honey; it's not a nice place to visit. But I might have to go there for a little while to look for your mom. If I go there, you and Esmeralda will stay with Grandma. Is that okay?"

Mag frowned, and fed another bit of her sandwich to the cat, who reached out through the front of the cage with one soft paw. "Why would Mommy be there?" she asked.

"She would not have gone there by choice, Mag – but she may not have had any choice," John said, agonizing over how to walk the line between the truth, and saying something that would frighten the child. This was a struggle he had undergone many times in the past few days.

"Oh," she replied, clearly unsatisfied with his answer, but willing to let it go for now.

Odie stood up, and slid over next to Maggie on the other side of the booth. "Finish your sandwich, sweetheart," she said. "Esmeralda doesn't need any more of it. Okay?" She hugged the little girl.

Maggie nodded. "How much longer will we be here, Daddy?" she asked.

"Not much longer. Our car will be ready soon, and then we have to drive a little farther…but not too much farther, okay?"

"Okay, Daddy," the little girl said.

John folded up the map and stared out the window, wondering how he could get news of what had happened to Rachel. He knew there was a chance that she had been condemned to death; it had happened before, to those who had seemed to subvert the government. As close as they were, though, he believed he would know if she were dead or in that much danger. He remembered how he had known when she went into labor with Maggie – she had been at the ministry center, and her water had broken unexpectedly, two weeks early. He had been at work, sitting at a drafting table, and suddenly he had felt a huge pain in his back, like nothing he'd ever felt in his life. In a flash, without even thinking, he knew it was Rachel – that she was going to give birth. He had rushed out of the office without even explaining to anyone where he was going, dialing Rachel's number as he went. What struck him most about the memory was that she hadn't been surprised that he knew. It seemed perfectly natural to her that he should feel, in his own body, such a momentous event that involved both of them.

The more he thought about it, the more sure he was that he would know if she were dead. Over the past few days, occasionally he had felt an inexplicable surge of hope, and he chose to believe it came from her. He felt it now, like a dove rising in his chest.

"Come on, everyone," he said, with a genuine smile. "Let's go!"

When Beth opened her eyes, she still could hardly believe how wonderful it was to have a private room of her own – she'd never experienced such a thing before in her life. It wasn't nice being in the hospital, of course, but now that she was out of Intensive Care, not only was her body healing from her injuries, her mind and soul were starting to heal from the fear and abuse she had endured all her life. She didn't know what would happen to her once she was out of the hospital, but something told her that she must try not to worry about that, and focus instead on absorbing the peace and care she was being given now. She knew she was a criminal, but it also occurred to her that it would be very strange for the government to care for her like this, and then kill or harm her. So she chose to allow the kindness of the nurses, and the quiet of the room, to permeate her mind. She had asked, once, if anyone knew what had happened to Rachel, but the nurse had put a finger to her lips, suggesting that they were not allowed to speak of it.

Today when she turned her head, there was a stranger sitting next to her bed. He wasn't a doctor; he was dressed in a beautifully tailored dark-blue suit, with a crisp white shirt and a lighter blue tie. He had silver hair and silver-rimmed glasses. He looked familiar to her somehow, though she wasn't sure why.

"Good afternoon, Bethany," he said. "How are you today?"

She reached for the remote control that raised and lowered her bed, and moved herself to a sitting position. "I'm all right," she said cautiously in her sweet, light voice. "Who are you?"

"I am Magistrate Jerry Cromwell," he said. He saw her flinch, and wondered if she had seen him or heard about him on the news, or if Rachel had said something to her about his visit to the ministry center. "Do you know who I am?" he asked.

"No…no," she replied. "But you're a magistrate. You must be here to punish me."

He reflected that a week ago, she wouldn't have been far from the mark. "Child," he said, in his kindest voice, "please let me assure you that I am not here to punish you. Quite the contrary. I am here to tell you that I have taken an interest in your case."

Beth's gray eyes, which reminded him so much of his sister's, were wide, staring at him. "Why?" she asked.

"Your story is an exceptional one," Cromwell said. "From what Rachel DeLine told me you have not been well-served by your government. I have spoken to the authorities at the orphanage you ran away from, as well. It is clear to me that you were socially alienated while you lived there, and that the adults in charge made no effort to ease your suffering. I know that you refused to convert to Christianity, but … let me ask you this, Bethany. Would you have considered living by the word of God if Rachel had asked you to?"

"Yes," Beth said, with no hesitation.

Cromwell nodded. "This is where the system failed you – and others, I suspect. We forgot that every child learns to understand the love of God only as it is shown to them in the love of those who take care of them. You had no means of understanding that love until it was translated to you in human form, by Rachel DeLine. This was not your fault. I feel that it is my responsibility to protect you – to make up for the wrongs done to you. It is true that I represent the church and the government. It is also true that I see where the law was blind to your needs.

"I can see that you are a good person, Beth. I know you have intelligence, and great strength of will and of heart. I would like to give you the chance to learn and grow in the ways of God, in a safe place, among people who will treat you kindly and fairly. For that reason, I have successfully petitioned the court to mitigate your sentence to five years' probation, rather than exile you to Judas Island. You will be released to my custody, and I will be your legal guardian. You will live with me and my wife, but our intention is to be your guardians and your mentors, not your jailors. We have a grown son, and we know how to be parents. We have love and care to give, Beth, and we would like the opportunity to give it to you."

Beth twisted the sheet between her hands, her mouth slightly open. "But--" she began.

"What is it, child?" Cromwell encouraged her.

"But my baby – will you love him, as well?"

Cromwell's heart squeezed painfully as he realized how innocent she was. "Bethany," he said gently, "I am afraid that your baby did not survive the fall from the cliff."

Beth put her hand against her belly. Her pregnancy had been so early when she discovered it; she felt no different now than she had when she went to Rachel.

"What about Rachel?" she asked. "What is happening to her?"

"Rachel…has been convicted of several counts against the law. She is on her way now to Judas Island," Cromwell said. It would have been unforgivably cruel to tell Beth about the public caning Rachel had to endure. She was too fragile. "Her friend Martha will be there, too," he added.

"So many people in trouble, because of me," Beth said mournfully.

"You mustn't blame yourself," Cromwell said firmly. "You were in trouble, and you looked for help. That is all." She nodded, and he watched her for a few minutes. "We were never able to find a DNA match for a father of your baby," he said. "We were therefore unable to bring the father of your child to justice."

"You never will," she said, but it was a simple statement of fact; there was nothing arrogant in her contradiction. "There is no father."

Cromwell still had no explanation for this piece of Beth's puzzle, and perhaps he never would. For now, it didn't matter.

"Beth, I would like to come visit you every day until you are out of the hospital, so you will not feel as if I am a stranger when you come to live with me," he said. "Is that all right?"

Her thin face came very close to a smile. "Yes," she replied. "okay."

━━━━━◦((◎))◦━━━━━

Rachel stood on the deck of the *S.S. Iscariot*, the ship that transported prisoners to Judas Island. Her hair whipped around her face in the moist sea wind as she waited her turn to be processed along with the other fifty-eight new arrivals. The six-hour sail to the island's only seaport, Macquarie Bay, had been frightening and unpleasant. The prisoners had been crowded together below deck, each with a hard wooden seat. The water had been rough. Rachel had offered comfort to fellow-passengers who were seasick or sick with fear. She had not betrayed her own pain, though every movement she made seemed to reopen the bleeding welts across her back and shoulders.

The line inched forward at a snail's pace. As Rachel entered the queue to step down to the pier, she noted the slimy, rotting boards, green with algae. The custodian who confirmed her name and identity did not seem to know who she was, which was something of a relief; she had been worried about seeming to be a "celebrity" prisoner. But it appeared she was just as faceless as all the rest of the incoming population. Rachel was given a package wrapped in brown paper; it contained, she was told, her regulation Judas Island prisoner uniform and sleeping clothes, a towel and washcloth, soap, toothpaste, and toothbrush. She was then sent to the next station, where she sat, and her head was shaved. This was done every month to both men and women. There was no vanity on Judas Island, and barely any identity. She tried not to mind as she felt her thick dark locks falling from her head. She focused instead on the bleak landscape around her – at 130 feet above sea level, very little could thrive on the island. The terrain was rocky, with only a few brave palm trees to break the monotony.

After all the prisoners were processed, they were led to the island's equivalent of a town square, where they were told to stand and wait. Everyone shivered in the cool, wet wind off the ocean. Many of the women were weeping over the loss of their hair, running their hands distractedly over their naked heads. After several minutes of waiting, a man in a gray uniform strode out and walked up on the dais in front of the prisoners. He was broad-chested and powerful, with a loud, deep voice that would have been audible even without the portable microphone he carried.

"Attention, prisoners," he boomed. "I am Ralph Seabrook, Governor of Judas Island. I am the absolute authority here. I am your warden, your jailor, your judge and jury. You answer to me. This colony of sinners and exiles is small. There are around 16,000 of you, give or take a few. You live or die depending upon how well you work together. And you will work. This island is, as you may have noticed, inhospitable. Despite this, we grow most of our own food here, in greenhouses and dedicated gardens. We also tend livestock. You will do your own cooking and housekeeping, in rotating shifts. Those of you with medical knowledge or skill will work in the sick ward. You will all take turns at the most humble tasks, and any who refuse or balk will be punished. You don't like the idea of emptying a bedpan, mucking the stable, slopping the pigs, or scrubbing the communal latrines? Well, you should have thought of that before you broke the law.

"Mandatory prayer services are held at 8 a.m., noon, and 6 p.m. The only excuse for not attending is confinement to the sick ward. You have flouted God's laws, and it is our duty to make sure you show proper respect to the God whom you have rebelled against. Because you have just arrived, you will be given the afternoon to find your bed in the barracks, and to orient yourself with the location of the latrines, mess hall, and chapel. Tonight after the 6:00 prayer meeting, you will meet with your barracks warden, who will interview you to determine any special skills you may have. I remind you, though, that skill or talent will not excuse you from serving your fellow-prisoners at the most humble level. Do not pretend to be someone you are not, in hopes of escaping hard work. Tomorrow morning you will be assigned to your first duty rotation. Any questions you have – and there should be none – can be addressed to your barracks warden. I will see all of you in two hours, at the prayer meeting."

His speech was received in perfect silence, and not a single head turned to watch him as he stepped down off the dais and strode away. As he left, ten gray-suited custodians walked out in front of the prisoners – five men and five women. One of the men announced: "You will be called by name, in alphabetical order. You will line up behind the custodian who calls your name. You will be led to your barracks."

It took less than five minutes for the new prisoners to be sorted. With nine other women, Rachel marched to the barracks reserved for last names A–F. The building was made of concrete, and had virtually no interior amenities…the floor was cement and the dormitory was bunk beds, ten to a room. Nobody had any privacy. The women who were already there did not make eye contact with the new arrivals. Rachel put her parcel of personal hygiene items on the rough blanket that covered her thin mattress, and then fell back into line to be shown where the latrines, mess hall, sick ward, and chapel were.

Away from the central square, the custodian seemed softer and more human. After she showed the women where the chapel was, she said, "The prayer meeting will start in half an hour. If you want, you can sit here until then. Some find it comforting to be in the chapel. In fact, it's always the case that if you finish your work early – and some do; you won't be punished for being quick, as long as you're thorough – you can come here for a bit of quiet."

Suddenly Rachel knew that the custodian was speaking directly to her. "Some of the new arrivals find it particularly comforting," she said, looking Rachel in the eye. Rachel's heart fluttered as she slid onto one of the hard pew benches. This woman knew who she was…and knew who Martha was. Rachel was careful not to react or respond in any way, but her heart surged with a song of gratitude. There was kindness, even here. God's mercy and grace were truly everywhere.

She knew she would see Martha again, and that she would have the chance to apologize to her dear friend. Hard work and suffering lay ahead, but as long as she had her life, she had hope. Her soul uplifted, she knelt on the stone floor of the barren chapel and began to pray.

THE END ... *of the beginning*

Epilogue

The view-screen on the wall was filled with animated shapes and colors generating a celestial appearance. Choir music swelled to a crescendo on the refrain of the hymn "Onward Christian Soldiers." As the music faded, the CGI visuals gave way to a good-looking man, who stood facing his audience, wearing a friendly look on his face. His eyes sparkled as he began to speak.

"Good evening, gentle folks. Tonight, the church wants you to know that our godly nation is safe, as we continue shining like a beacon for the rest of this dark and troubled world. I am Gordon Whitfield, your herald of good news on this blessed evening. And, I bring you a special report from The Quorum of Elders tonight.

"Our sacred vigilance continues with the pursuit of an illegal video that has gone 'viral' in cyberspace. I refer to a blasphemous speech of a criminal woman at her tribunal – virtually challenging, even defying the infallibility of the Holy Bible as the basis for our Christian Law and Order in this country! I remind all good citizens of our land that even viewing this video clip makes you guilty of heresy.

Anyone who is involved in spreading this viral video on the web is violating the law. And if you become aware of someone engaged in such subversive activity, if you do not immediately report them to our Law Stewards, then you are guilty of a crime! All such rebellious perpetuation of this blasphemy will cease, at once; or else violators will be arrested and punished to the full extent of the penalty code!"

"On a more peaceable, yet also victorious report," the herald began again, "the 'Natural Law of Eden' was obeyed and celebrated, today. Dozens of reclaimed souls, formerly enslaved to abomination, were joyously engaged in holy matrimony, as man and wife – the way God intended. They were united in this blessing of normal life and natural love before 20,000 witnesses at the Temple Square, in Colorado Springs. Christ is smiling.

"Be assured, gentle spirits, one day soon we will fully be the pure and devout Christian nation of our manifest destiny!"

The herald's handsome face broke into full smiling radiance. "This is Gordon Whitfield, on behalf of the holy governance shepherding this Christian nation, wishing you a blessed night of safety and peace."

AFTERWORD

I am glad to dedicate this book to all Pro-Family, Pro-choice, Pro-Faith members of the *Religious Coalition for Reproductive Choice* **[RCRC]** who engage the critical struggle in this American 'culture war'. So, this work is also for Planned Parenthood, and NARAL, and all those who contend daily against the "Christian Right"; as the misguided efforts of those religionists attempt to return American women to earlier eras - when they were subordinate to patriarchal societies – when women were oppressed by hypocritical standards of sexual purity – when women were held incapable of real wisdom regarding <u>their own</u> wombs. Heaven forbid such trampling ever again of any woman's *inalienable, God-given rights to reproductive freedom and liberty!* {Clearly, God has certainly given women the accompanying responsibility for the morality of their own wombs.}

I want to acknowledge my debt to classic American authors Ray Bradbury, "*Farenheit 451*", and Margaret Atwood, "*The Handmaids Tale*" -- for their influence upon this entire genre of cautionary tales.

I thank my wife and sons for their understanding support of me in this deeply personal pursuit. Also, I am grateful to Joan Rogers for her invaluable assistance in this creative enterprise. Finally, I have been blessed by the encouragement of several friends along the way [you know who you are!] and mentors in the faith, whose influences helped give shape to my creativity.

Faith, hope and charity – remain; but the greatest of these is LOVE.

"WHEN THE POWER OF LOVE OVERCOMES THE LOVE OF POWER, THE WORLD WILL KNOW PEACE." -- Jimi Hendrix

www.ingramcontent.com/pod-product-compliance
Lightning Source LLC
Chambersburg PA
CBHW051237050326
40689CB00007B/956